*He was Kay_____ n if
he pretended __ __ ___ _____.*

"You should be very afraid of me."

Her voice was hesitant. "Why?"

"Because I'm a monster."

"What do you mean?"

"I'm a trained killing machine. That it was my job is no excuse."

"Stop doing this to yourself," she said. "The world is full of people who've been pushed into the same situation. That doesn't make any of you monsters."

"No? Then what the hell does it make us?"

"People," she said flatly. "Ordinary people."

"Don't trust me," he said. "Don't ever, ever trust me."

"I already trust you."

He swore and jumped up from his chair, unable to hold still another minute. Finally he came to a halt as far as he could get from her in the room. He hoped letting it out had scared her good. For her own protection.

Then he felt a touch on his forearm.

"Clint," she said softly.

Damn, it was too late. Turning, he wrapped her in his arms and pulled her tightly to him, crushing her mouth beneath his.

Because, heaven help him, he needed the human touch. The human warmth. The feeling that he was still, at heart, good enough for someone.

Dear Reader,

It is so sad to me that a subject I first picked up in *Lost Warriors* years ago is once again relevant, and probably more so than ever. The struggles our soldiers face when they return home are enormous. Some may never be able to find peace. And, of course, domestic abuse continues as a plague.

I write to tell a good story, not to preach. Part of that storytelling for me must involve the exploration of the human heart. It is how we find each other, thus finding shelter amid life's storms, that endlessly fascinates me. How do two people cross a long, uncertain bridge to the point of trust where love can blossom?

Each of us finds his or her own way to that place, and the paths are varied. The journey to the oasis we call love is endlessly fascinating, endlessly touching.

Most of us have sorrow or pain in our past. Finding comfort and love is probably one of the most important journeys we take. For only a heart filled with love has love to give. I hope you enjoy this tale of two devastatingly wounded hearts as they strive for peace and happiness.

Hugs,

Rachel

RACHEL LEE

Her Hero in Hiding

ROMANTIC
SUSPENSE

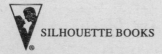

SILHOUETTE BOOKS

Recycling programs for this product may not exist in your area.

ISBN-13: 978-0-373-27681-3

HER HERO IN HIDING

Visit Silhouette Books at www.cHarlequin.com

Printed in U.S.A.

Books by Rachel Lee

RACHEL LEE

was hooked on writing by the age of twelve, and practiced her craft as she moved from place to place all over the United States. This *New York Times* bestselling author now resides in Florida and has the joy of writing full time.

Her bestselling Conard County miniseries (see www.conardcounty.com) has won the hearts of readers worldwide, and it's no wonder, given her own approach to life and love. As she says, "Life is the biggest romantic adventure of all—and if you're open and aware, the most marvelous things are just waiting to be discovered."

To all the heroes in hiding from pasts
they struggle to make peace with.

Chapter 1

Snow flurries began to blow before Clint Ardmore left Conard City with his truckload of supplies. By the time he reached the county road leading to his ranch, it became apparent that winter was arriving. Big flakes whipped about in the wind, threatening a whiteout later when the temperatures dropped enough to make the snow nearly as fine as sand. As it was, the flakes reflected his low beams sufficiently to make the already dark afternoon seem darker.

Winter pleased him. He liked the cold, the snow, the isolation it brought to his ranch. Not even the most determined salesman or missionary would try to make it up the road to his house, and the neighbors to whom he leased his land for their own stock were undoubtedly pulling the last of them in. Soon his ranch would become exactly what he wanted it to be—a hermitage he left only out of necessity.

At least that was his cheerful expectation until he caught sight of a gray figure staggering alongside the road.

Hell, no one ought to be out here on foot. Cussing under his breath, he jammed on his brakes and pulled over. The snow was only just beginning to stick, so he didn't skid. Some drunk, no doubt, lost in the middle of nowhere. But whatever this person was doing out here, there was no way he could be left to wander alone in this weather. From here to the nearest ranch—his—it was another ten miles.

Clint climbed out and slammed the truck door. The wind had taken on a nasty bite, presaging a deadly night for unprotected humans.

Still cussing—he possessed quite an amazing vocabulary of cuss words in several languages—he stomped back toward the staggering figure in gray. The snow continued to swirl, thick enough to be almost fog-like. He really needed this, he thought. Now he would have to drive back to town in this damn storm to make sure this idiot didn't freeze to death out here.

It wasn't until he was only a few steps away that he realized the idiot was a woman and, worse, a woman dressed only in a gray sweatshirt and pants. And when she lifted her head at his approach, he saw a shiner that would have looked appropriate on a boxer, not on a tiny woman with straggly blond hair and blue eyes the size of saucers.

At least they became saucer-size when they saw him.

Well, he could kind of understand that. He was a large man, well over six feet, and years in Special Ops had given him a need to stay in shape that wouldn't quit even though he'd left the military well behind him. Then there was his face. The faces on Mt. Rushmore looked less stony.

Too bad.

"Hey, lady!" he called. "You're going to freeze!"

She staggered another step, then turned and started to run. Only she couldn't quite run, because her feet didn't seem to be cooperating, and moments later she tumbled facedown on the shoulder.

At once he raced to her side and squatted. "Lady..."

"Go away!" she cried. "Get away from me!"

"I won't hurt you," he said, making his voice as gentle as when he talked to his horses. Not exactly second nature, but he knew how.

"No! No! Get away from me."

Another time, another place, he might have been happy to oblige. But not out here. Not even on a sunny day. Not when she had a black eye like that, which might mean a bad concussion.

"Easy," he said quietly. "Easy. I won't hurt you, I swear. But you'll freeze out here."

Then he reached out to help her up and realized he might as well have tried to lift an angry mountain lion. She started fighting the instant she felt his hands, kicking and swinging and trying to scratch him.

Experience came to his aid. Keeping his hold as gentle as he could, keeping her back to his chest to minimize the damage to himself, he lifted her. "Shh," he said soothingly near her ear. "Shh. I'm just going to take you to a doctor."

"No! No!" She wriggled wildly. "He'll find me! He'll find me!" There was no mistaking the terror and desperation in her voice.

"All right, then," he agreed gently, all the while wondering why he was making such an insane promise. "All right. But how about you come home with me and get warm? You'll freeze out here."

"I don't care! He'll find me!"

"Nobody's going to find you at my place, I swear. I promise you'll be safe…."

He kept murmuring soothingly, taking care to keep his grip without hurting her. She fought a little longer, but she didn't have a whole lot of strength left, and soon enough she began to sag.

He shifted her a bit, so his hold was more comfortable, then swung her up and began carrying her toward his truck. A car drove by, slowing down, but he barely glanced at it before it sped up. He didn't recognize it, so it didn't belong to the only other rancher on this road before it dead-ended. He felt a fleeting suspicion, but dismissed it. If someone were following her in a car, he would certainly have caught her long since. Probably someone visiting. Not that he cared.

"No doctor," she said again, but her blue eyes had begun to look hazy.

"No doctor," he agreed. "Just a warm fire and some food."

Then she said something that tore at his heart. Her huge blue eyes focused on his face, and she said, "You're not him."

Then she passed out.

Kay Young returned to woozy consciousness to find she was lying on a soft sofa beneath a heap of quilts near a cheerfully burning fire. Dimly she realized it felt odd to be warm, because she had been cold for so long, so very long. But she no longer felt frozen to the bone.

When she tried to move, however, everything hurt, from her head to her feet, and she groaned. The pounding in her head alone nauseated her, and the world around her spun.

At once she heard a sound; then a stranger with a hard, harsh face was squatting beside her. "Shh," he said softly. "You're safe here. I promise. Shh. You might have a concussion."

"I have to go," she said weakly, struggling against pain, a swimming world and the quilts. "He'll find me. I can't let him find me." *Run!* The word shrieked in her brain, burned into every cell. *Escape! Flee!*

"Easy, lady," he said quietly. "Easy. You're hurt. No one's going to find you here. No one."

"He will," she said desperately, terror clutching at her insides with bony, knifing fingers. "He always finds me."

"Easy," he said again. "There's a blizzard outside. No one's getting here tonight, not even the doctor. I know because I tried."

"Doctor? I don't need a doctor! I've got to get away."

"There's nowhere to go tonight," he said levelly. "Nowhere. And if I thought you could stand, I'd take you to a window and show you."

But even as she tried once more to push away the quilts, she remembered something else—this man had been gentle when he'd found her beside the road, even when she had kicked and clawed. He hadn't hurt her. Not like her ex-boyfriend.

Terror receded just a bit. She looked at him, *really* looked at him, and though his face might have been granite, she detected signs of true concern there. True kindness.

The terror eased another notch, and she let her head sag on the pillow. "He always finds me," she whispered.

"Not here. Not tonight. That much I can guarantee."

And she believed him. Oh, God, she believed him. "Thank you," she murmured finally.

"I heated up some broth. Let's see if you can hold a little bit of it down. Do you feel sick to your stomach?"

"Yes."

"Maybe a couple of crackers first, then. After that we can try broth. I'll be right back."

She watched him straighten, amazed at his sheer size. Everything about him looked as if it might have been carved out of the nearby mountains. As he walked away from her, other things began to penetrate. She was in a warm room, a cozy room, with walls that looked like a log cabin. The furnishings were sparse but colorful, and they looked comfortable. The fire blazed merrily in a stone fireplace.

Nothing, absolutely *nothing,* about this place seemed in any way related to her tormentor or her experience since…since when? She didn't even know how long she had been in hell, how long ago she had begun to fear men. All men. Everything in her head was a jumble.

Oh God. She allowed her eyes to close, let her aching body relax at last. Oh God. Maybe she had truly escaped.

Maybe.

"Crackers?"

Her savior had returned with a small plate holding a dozen soda crackers. Only then did she realize, nauseated or not, that she was famished. Moving gingerly, she pushed herself up against the arm of the couch. He didn't try to touch her, not even to help. That seemed like a good sign.

She held the plate on her lap and nibbled at a cracker.

"I'm Clint Ardmore," he said.

"Kay Young," she answered, surprised at how weak she sounded. "May I have some water?"

"I can't believe I forgot that." He hopped up immediately from the roughly hewn coffee table on which he'd been sitting. "Would you prefer something carbonated? Maybe ginger ale or club soda?"

"Ginger ale, please."

He vanished once again, returning a minute later with a tall glass of soda. "I didn't put ice in it," he said. "I figured you need to warm up, and this is already chilled from the fridge."

"That's great. Thanks." She sipped it with relief, feeling it wet her mouth and burn a little. Her stomach liked it, and soon she was eating another cracker.

"Is it settling?"

"Very well." More ginger ale, another cracker. Somehow he no longer seemed frightening. But how could she be frightened of a man who was practically hovering in concern, a man who had given her his name without asking hers?

"You have one hell of a shiner," he said.

She looked at him. Again that granite face reflected genuine concern.

"He hit me," she said simply. Hard. Multiple times. But she didn't add all that.

"I could have guessed that," he said. "I should call the sheriff."

"No!" Panic erupted again, and he grabbed the soda from her hand right before she spilled it. "No! He'll kill me if he finds me!"

"Easy. Easy. Okay. No sheriff for now. Nothing tonight. Nobody can move in this storm anyway. You just rest. We can talk about everything tomorrow."

Tomorrow. For the first time in what felt like an eternity, she dared to believe there would be one. "I'm sorry," she said finally, staring at the crackers that still rested in her lap.

"No need. I can tell you've been through hell. Just take it easy. You're safe now."

And she believed him. For now, anyway. She looked at him gratefully as her panic subsided, then resumed eating.

"I'm still dizzy," she remarked. "On and off."

"That sounds like a concussion. You might be dizzy for a while."

It was then she noticed that her sweatshirt had turned dark green. Another shiver of panic. "What happened to my clothes?" Her gaze darted to his face, and for a moment the world turned into a carousel before settling again.

He frowned. "You don't remember?"

"Remember what?"

"Your clothes were wet from the snow. I helped you change into one of my sweat suits. You said it was okay."

Something far from pleasant started dancing along nerves that were already on the edge of shrieking from pain and terror. "I don't remember."

He swore. "Well, that settles it. You're seeing a doctor tomorrow. If you won't go to him, I'll get him to come to you. This sounds like a really bad concussion."

"He might find me," she said again, plunging back into the nightmare. "He said he was going to kill me!"

"No one will find you. I'll figure out something."

"Oh God, oh God…" And then she started to cry.

A fine freaking kettle of fish, Clint thought as he banged around in his kitchen, slamming pots a little harder than necessary as he tried to decide what the *hell* he was going to cook for himself, because he hadn't eaten all day. A terrified, injured woman in his living room, crying her eyes out, looking for all the world as if she'd been beaten and maybe tortured, who couldn't even remember letting him help her into dry clothes, who wouldn't let him take her to a doctor, not that he could anyway in the midst of this blizzard….

And all he wanted was his peace and solitude. He had a book to write, a deadline to meet, and he'd had enough of the real world to last him a lifetime. Enough so that it had stuck firmly in his craw and simply wouldn't be dislodged. And now the real world had landed on his doorstep, invaded his solitude and brought all its problems with it.

But what the hell was he supposed to do? A day, he promised himself. Two at most. He would convince her to talk to the sheriff, to see the doctor, and he would send her safely on her way to wherever she was from, where she would have family and friends and others who were far better suited to helping her through this than a crusty hermit like himself.

Finally he gave up all thought of creating some culinary masterpiece, his one indulgence, and settled instead on cocoa and some cinnamon rolls he'd bought earlier. He made enough for two in case she thought she could eat.

What kind of man would treat a woman that way and leave her so terrified? But he knew. He really didn't need to ask the question, because he'd known men like that. One of the things that lodged in his craw. He'd worked with them. They would get all messed up on the job, then take it home with them and treat their wives and girlfriends, and sometimes even their kids, like enemy combatants. He knew them too well. And he wished he didn't. So what if they were a minority?

At least *he* had the sense to realize that his training and experience had made him unfit for society. But God almighty, now he had that waif in the next room depending on him, and all that stuff about honor and duty and protecting the defenseless was rising up like the opening curtain on another nightmare.

Another cuss word escaped him under his breath. He stacked everything on a tray and carried it into the other room.

Kay was lying on the couch, her eyes closed, so still she might have been dead. His heart nearly stopped. He knew the dangers of concussion all too well.

"Kay?"

He set the tray on the coffee table and felt concern clamp his chest in a vise. "Kay?" he repeated.

No answer. Did he dare touch her? If she was unconscious, she would never know, but if she woke with a stranger touching her, he might set off her panic again.

"Kay!" Loudly. A command.

Then, to his infinite relief, her eyes fluttered open. "Kay," he repeated, more quietly.

Slowly, very slowly, her gaze tracked to his face. "Mmm?" she asked drowsily.

"I brought cinnamon buns and cocoa. Do you want to eat something more?"

"I...yes." She tried to push herself up a little more, then squeezed her eyes shut. "The world keeps moving."

"It'll stop. Just wait a few seconds before you open your eyes again."

She followed his suggestion, and when she looked at him again, her gaze remained steady.

"Cocoa?" he asked. "Or a bun? Or should I get the chicken broth?"

She hesitated, then said, "Cocoa sounds better."

Pushing the tray to one side, he sat on the low table and faced her, passing her a mug. She cradled it in both hands, though he couldn't tell whether she was seeking the warmth or worried it might spin away. Then she sipped, and her expression told him it was okay. He didn't need to run for a bucket. The cocoa would stay down.

Relieved, he reached for his own mug. "So what happened?" he asked finally.

"My...boyfriend."

His ire rose. "Your *boyfriend* did this to you?"

"My ex. Yes." She sighed and closed her eyes a moment. Her hands trembled, and he almost reached to take the mug from her.

"I can't remember much," she offered hesitantly. "It's all mixed up."

"That's okay." He tried to sound reassuring. "Concussions do that." And trauma, but he didn't add that. What was the point? Words wouldn't change her situation.

"Thank you," she said finally.

"For what? I haven't done much."

The corners of her mouth quivered, a sight that distressed him. Crying women were not his forte.

"For saving me," she said simply. "Thank you for saving me."

That was when he knew his troubles were just beginning.

Chapter 2

Wrapped around the mug of cocoa, Kay's fingers began to warm. At first they burned and tingled painfully, but then they began to feel normal again. She sipped the hot cocoa gratefully and glanced at the man who had retreated to the easy chair on the other side of the coffee table. Somehow that retreat made him seem even safer.

"Where am I?" she asked finally.

"On my ranch," he replied. "About twenty-five miles outside of Conard City, Wyoming."

"Wyoming?" The thought shocked her. How had she come to be so far from home? Had she really been trapped for that long? "I live in Texas!"

His face seemed to stiffen a bit, but she wasn't a hundred percent sure. Reading him was like reading runes—apparently you had to know the language. "That's a long way," he said finally. "You want to tell me what happened?"

"I can't…right now." Her mind recoiled from the memories, unwilling to remember the nightmare. "I can't," she said again, her heart accelerating.

"That's okay," he said soothingly. "I don't need to know. It can wait."

That was a pretty generous statement coming from a man who had picked her up off the roadside and welcomed her into his home. She felt she had to offer him something. "I ran," she said finally. "We were at a rest stop and he thought I was unconscious, and when he went inside, I ran. I ran…" Her voice trailed off, and she closed her eyes.

"You ran a helluva distance," he said. "The nearest rest stop I can think of is about nine miles from where I found you."

"I run marathons," she said simply.

A soft oath escaped him. She looked at him then, and there was no mistaking the anger on his face. She wanted to shrink and hide, but there was no place to go, not now.

But moments later his face settled back into impassivity. Of course, he wasn't mad at *her,* she thought. Not like *him.* This was a different man, one who was trying to help her. He had been nothing but kind.

"So you're from Texas," he said presently. "I spent some time there, years ago, mostly in Killeen."

She started. "Really? That's where I'm from."

"Small world sometimes."

"Or very big." Her words seemed to hang on the air. She wasn't quite sure what she'd meant, except that maybe now the world seemed more threatening than it had before Kevin. Into her small world, evil had come, a kind of evil she had once thought would never intersect with her life.

"Yeah," he said presently, "it can be."

As if he understood. Perhaps he did.

"I...tried to get away from him," she offered. God, it was so hard to speak of it. "He kept following. I moved three times, and he found me every time, and now..." Her voice broke. She couldn't continue.

"You're away from him now."

"Yes. Now." She squeezed her eyes shut. "But for how long?"

For a long time there was no sound but the crackling fire and keening wind. Then he asked, "You moved three times? Different towns?"

"Different states."

He swore. She jerked her head back, feeling the inescapable stab of fear, then relaxed when he didn't move a muscle.

"That's bad," he said quietly.

"You can't hide anymore," she said. "Not anymore. Not with the Internet."

"So it seems. And restraining orders might as well be written on toilet paper."

"You can't get one when you move to a new state. The judge asks where your proof is that he'll follow you. So the last time I didn't even try."

He shook his head. "By the time the restraining order is broken, you're already in too much trouble for it to do you much good."

"Yeah. I've learned that the hard way." She bit her lip, still clinging to the cocoa mug as if it were a lifeline. "That's why I don't want to let anyone know where I am. He'll find me. He always does."

He nodded but didn't say anything. She watched his stony face, trying to read something there, but couldn't. He was a man, and she ought to be frightened because Kevin had indelibly taught her that no matter how nice a guy might seem at first, he could turn into a monster.

But Clint Ardmore didn't know her yet. She was new to him, so regardless of what kind of man he might be, it was still too early to have to fear him. And she would be gone before it reached that point.

At least that was what she needed to believe.

"Okay," he said at last. "I won't even call the sheriff. At least not tonight. We can talk more about it when you're feeling a bit better."

She hated that he sounded grudging, but there was no way she could ignore his concession, even if he didn't want to make it. "Thank you."

"As to this concussion...I'm no doctor, but there's one thing I know for sure. I can't let you sleep too long or too deeply tonight, so you'd better make up your mind that I'm going to be waking you often. And if that means shaking you, I *will* shake you."

She didn't want to be touched. Not by anyone. Fear clogged her throat, even though she understood the sense of what he was saying. "I...only if you have to."

"Only if I can't wake you by banging a pot next to your ear." Then he surprised her by lifting one corner of his mouth in an almost-smile. "Can you live with that?"

"I think so."

"Don't worry about attacking me," he added, the smile deepening enough to seem almost real. "You already tried that and didn't even put a scratch on me. So if you wake up frightened and strike out, it's okay."

That was meant to calm her? Yet in some odd way it did. "I don't remember attacking you."

"Most likely not. You were pretty out of it, between the concussion and hypothermia. But yeah, you tried to defend yourself even when you were weaker than a newborn kitten."

He seemed to like that she'd defended herself, although she couldn't imagine why. It *did,* however, make her feel better about herself. Even totally out of it, she'd put up a fight.

"Anyway," he went on, "the blizzard alone should be enough protection for tonight. But I'll make sure everything's locked up tight. Don't usually have to bother, but..." He left the thought unfinished and shrugged.

"Thank you." It *would* make her feel safer. "And thank you for your hospitality."

Now *he* looked distinctly uncomfortable. "I wouldn't have left a stray cat out there tonight. Would have been inhuman."

Now how did he mean that? She wished she could peer behind the emotionless facade of his face and get an inkling of how this man thought.

No, maybe not. Maybe she didn't really want to know what went on inside him. Tomorrow she would be gone, as soon as the blizzard let up enough and...

"Oh my God!" The words escaped her before she could stop them.

"What?"

"I just realized. How am I going to get out of here?"

"I'll take you to a bus or something when the roads clear."

"No, you don't understand! He took my purse. I don't have any ID, no credit card, no money! Oh, God, I'm trapped!"

Just as she started to spiral into fresh panic, he stopped her with one word of command.

"No."

She gaped at him. "What?"

"I said no. Don't do it. Don't wind yourself up. I can help you out with all of that. Trust me, you'll be on your way again as soon as possible."

From something in the way he said it, she believed him. He didn't want her here any more than she wanted to be here.

It was a weird kind of hope, but it was a hope she had to cling to.

Besides, she reminded herself, she'd always found a way to run before. Always. She just needed to wait to gather her strength and lose the mental fog that seemed to be slowing her brain.

She finally ate one of the rolls he offered, and even downed another cup of cocoa. The heat from the fire began to penetrate enough that she threw back the quilt and lay there in the oversized green sweats he had put her into. "My toes are burning."

He looked at her feet. "I'm not surprised. They were getting close to frostbite. But they look a healthy pink now."

She hadn't even considered all the horrible dangers when she had taken her chance to flee the car wearing nothing but her grey sweats and running shoes into a cold Wyoming afternoon. With absolutely no thought of what she should do or where she should turn, she had fled. She hadn't even risked trying to hide at the rest stop in the hopes that someone else would drive in and she could seek help.

"I guess running like that wasn't my smartest move."

"I don't know, but from what little you've told me, it may have been your *only* move."

"It seemed like it." Then she stole another glance at him. "I couldn't have made it much farther, could I?"

"I don't know. Willpower can sometimes accomplish near miracles. I'm glad we'll never have to find out, though."

At least not this time, she thought miserably. Kevin had grown bigger than life in her mind, more like a nightmare monster than a mere man. "You know what I can't understand?"

"What's that?"

"Why he keeps coming after me. Why can't he just let me go? I go as far away as I can get, and he still comes looking. I just don't get it!"

He shook his head. "I'm no psychologist. I don't get why he abused you in the first place."

"I can understand that better than him tracking me like this. I mean, he has a temper. He blows up. At first I was even able to forgive him. But…" She shook her head. "I don't get it."

He suddenly leaned forward, almost like a striking snake, and she shrank back instinctively.

"Don't ever," he said, "*ever, forgive someone who hits you. Ever.*"

She blinked, wondering what the hell was behind that, but then he leaned back and reached for his own mug as if he hadn't just vented that moment of passion. "Creeps like him," Clint said quietly, "once they cross that line, they just keep on crossing it like it was never there."

That much made sense. She nodded. "I guess you're right."

"I know I'm right." His gray eyes seemed to burn. "You can't erase the lines and then draw them again. The lines get blurred, and it almost never works. Especially if they get a taste for power or inflicting fear."

She felt her mouth sag open a little and quickly closed it. They were definitely having a discussion about something that reached far beyond Kevin, but she couldn't imagine what it was.

He rose quickly, mug in hand. "Want more?"

"I'm fine, thanks."

He headed swiftly for the kitchen, as if he wanted to get away from the whole conversation.

Not that she could blame him. She didn't exactly like it herself.

She lay there, mug in her hands, staring into the dancing fire, wondering more about her rescuer than she should. He seemed like a troubled man, and that made her uneasy.

But, she reminded herself again, she would be out of here as soon as she could manage after the storm passed.

In a day or so she would never have to see Clint Ardmore again. There was absolutely no point in trying to figure him out, not when she was going to shake him off her heels like the dust along the road of what was evidently going to become a permanent flight.

God. She wanted to weep, but the tears wouldn't come. Just as well. She didn't want to annoy her rescuer. But how the dickens was she ever going to get out of this mess? The one and only time she'd managed to get Kevin charged and thrown into jail, he'd gotten out in less than two years.

Apparently it was a far worse crime to kick your dog than beat your girlfriend. And it was a lot harder to prove domestic abuse, too. The second time she'd gone to the cops, Kevin had denied he was even in town. Since he lived four states away and hadn't done anything stupid, like buy gas with a credit card or rent a hotel room, the prosecutor had shrugged and dismissed the charge for lack of proof that tied Kevin to the assault. There were so many more important cases to pursue, after all.

The wind hammered the windows, making them rattle behind the curtains, and she looked around uneasily. Kevin had to know she had taken off running. He might have wondered if she had been picked up along the road, maybe by a long-distance trucker, but he probably wouldn't have wondered for long. The roads had been deserted, maybe because of the approaching storm, and the stop had been a brief one, brief enough that she had heard him shouting her name in the distance as she hid in a thicket of trees before dashing off again.

No, he wouldn't know which way she'd gone, but he'd probably figured out pretty quickly that she wasn't running along the highway. That would have been the first thing he checked.

So he might stay in the area, looking for her.

Regardless, she couldn't afford to have her name turn up in a police blotter or anywhere else he could find it by means of the Internet.

So what now?

The question loomed darkly, without answers. Finally she pushed it away, promising herself she would think about it in the morning, after the throbbing in her head eased and her thoughts cleared.

Because right now even *she* could tell she was far from being at her best.

A male voice called her name sharply, and she started. "What?"

She looked around and saw Clint sitting on the coffee table again. The mug was no longer in her hands.

"You've been sleeping about half an hour," he said.

"I didn't even realize I'd dozed off."

He nodded. "You're exhausted. But we still have to watch out for that concussion. Sorry, but I'm going to make this a long night for you."

"I understand." She did. Moving carefully, she tried to sit up, but the room tilted and spun so much that she had to close her eyes.

"Do you need something?"

"The bathroom. But I'm dizzy."

"Let me help you. Keep your eyes closed."

She expected him to take her arm, help her to her feet and guide her. But instead he lifted her from the couch like a doll and carried her. She definitely did *not* like that. She hated being reminded that he was so much stronger than she was. It was all she could do not to fight him as fear grabbed her anew.

But then he let her feet slide to the floor and steadied her with an arm around her waist.

"Wait a minute," he said, "then open your eyes."

She did as he suggested, and when she opened her eyes the room appeared stable. It was a small bathroom, just the essentials, with little extra room.

"This is the most dangerous room in the house," he reminded her. "Don't move quickly, don't turn or tip your head, and hang on to something every time you move. If you get dizzy, just holler. I'll be right outside the door."

"Thanks."

With care and extreme caution, she managed to take care of her needs, but when it came time to walk to the door, she felt unsteady enough to call out.

"Clint?"

He entered swiftly, offering immediate support. "Let me carry you," he said this time. "The sweatpants could trip you."

So it hadn't just been an exercise of male dominance when he had lifted her before. Relieved, she didn't argue, and this time she felt no fear when he picked her up. He laid her back on the sofa as if she were fragile enough to shatter.

"How's your head?"

"Still aching," she admitted.

"I'm sorry I can't give you aspirin. But with a concussion, that could be dangerous. And I don't have anything else."

"That's all right. It's reminding me I'm still alive."

Something flickered across his face, so quickly that she couldn't quite read it. She suspected that stoniness would make him a difficult man to deal with. At least with Kevin she had always known just what kind of trouble was on the horizon, even if she couldn't stop it or escape it.

"Can I get you anything?" he asked. "Food? Soup? A drink?"

"I'm really thirsty," she admitted. "Would you mind? Ginger ale?"

"Not a problem."

She let her head rest against the pillow, listening to the hammering storm outside. The thick log walls protected them from most of it, but through the closed windows she could hear the keening of the wind, and sometimes the glass rattled before the strength of it. Not even Kevin, she assured herself, could be out looking for her in this. Thank God.

But what was she going to do when it passed? With no identification or money, or even her debit card, how could she start running again? Fear and grief grabbed her in as tight a grip as the throbbing headache, and for a few seconds she couldn't even draw a breath. Never before had he trapped her quite this effectively. Always before she'd been able to gather enough resources to run again.

Well, she would find a way, she promised herself. She always had before.

"You're going to be all right."

She moved her eyes slowly until she could see Clint standing beside her, holding out a tall glass of ginger ale. For a moment he seemed to swim, then the world stabilized again. "Thanks." She reached out and took the glass, and only then realized that she needed to sit up straighter to drink.

Clint apparently saw the problem at the same instant she realized it. He took the glass back and bent to help her sit up against the pillow. "I guess I must be tired," he said. "Missing the obvious."

"Do you never miss the obvious?"

"I miss very little." An edge in his tone warned her away, though from what she didn't know. Silently, she accepted the glass back.

He rounded the coffee table and sat in the easy chair on the other side. A book lay open on the end table, and he picked it up to start reading again. Apparently he didn't feel like conversing.

Which ordinarily would have been fine, but Kay discovered her own thoughts scared her. She didn't want to be alone inside her own head. But how could you converse with a man who was doing a passable imitation of a brick wall?

A native caution when dealing with men kept her silent. She didn't want to irritate this man. From his size and strength, he could present an even bigger threat than Kevin, even though he hadn't done a thing to indicate he might be that kind of person.

She sipped her ginger ale, and a sigh escaped her. At once he spoke.

"Are you all right?"

"Just unhappy with my thoughts."

"I can understand."

Maybe he could. She dared to look at him again and found he had set the book aside.

"I guess I should apologize," he said finally, his tone level, his face unchanging. "I've been a hermit for a while. By choice. I seem to have lost the social graces."

"I'm not asking for social graces," she said truthfully. "You've been very kind to a stranger. I don't want to intrude more than necessary. It's just that my thoughts keep running in circles. Unhappy circles."

"You've certainly got enough to be unhappy about."

It might have been a question, a suggestion or an end to the subject. From what she had seen of him so far, she guessed it was probably a signal to end the discussion. So she took another sip of ginger ale and focused her attention on the fire. She could take a hint. In fact, she was probably hyper-alert to hints, thanks to Kevin.

But Clint surprised her by not returning to his book. "I suggest you plan to stay here for a couple of days." The invitation sounded grudging, and she looked askance at him.

"Why? You said you're a hermit by choice."

"Maybe so, but it seems to me you need some time, some *safe* time, to make plans and figure out your next move. You can't just run out of here the instant the storm ends. And I can provide the safety you need."

He said the last with such calm confidence that she wondered who the hell he was. Or what he had been before becoming a hermit. Not even the most sympathetic cop had ever promised her that much. No, they had been full of warnings and advice, most of which included getting as far away as possible as fast as possible.

"Kevin," she said finally, "is like a bomb. There's no telling when he'll go off, and anyone in the vicinity is probably at risk."

"I've dealt with bombs, and I've dealt with worse than Kevin." A frown dragged at the corners of his mouth but didn't quite form. "Trust me, I can keep you safe."

"The *cops* couldn't keep me safe."

"They couldn't be there round the clock," he said flatly. "And cops don't have my training."

She hesitated, then just blurted it out. "Who are you? *What* are you?"

His gaze grew distant, as if he could see through the walls and well past the blizzard beyond. A shiver ran through her. "I was special ops for nearly twenty years. And I was good at it. *Very* good."

She didn't know how to respond to that. Should she congratulate him? Admire him? But no. Something in that rigid face told a very different story. "I don't want you to have to go back to that. To relive it."

At that the facade cracked, and he looked startled. Then the stone returned. "Sometimes," he said after a moment, "you don't have a choice."

Chapter 3

The night passed without further conversation. Either weariness or the concussion, or a combination of both, kept causing her to nod off. Every half hour or so, he woke her, then let her fall back to sleep.

Then, finally, she knew it had to be morning because she awoke to the smell of frying bacon. The aroma made her mouth water, and she realized she was ravenous. When she pushed herself cautiously upright, she was delighted to realize the room no longer spun. The crazy carousel was gone.

Her head still ached, but not as badly, and most of the pain she felt now was in her cheek and around her black eye. There were aches and pains from running in the cold, from the other blows Kevin had heaped on her, but nothing she couldn't ignore.

Moving carefully, pulling the legs of the sweatpants up as she walked, she made her way to the bathroom and freshened up a bit. Then, upon returning to the living room, she pulled one of the heavy curtains back and looked out on the still-raging blizzard.

It was early yet, still dark outside, but even so, she could tell visibility probably didn't extend much past the porch railing she could barely see, buried as it was in snowy drifts and further concealed by wildly blowing snow. Even after the storm passed, just getting out the front door would probably prove to be a challenge.

"Good morning."

Startled, she almost jumped but managed to remember her unsteadiness in time. Gripping the window frame, she turned to see Clint standing in the doorway of his kitchen. "Good morning."

He gave a half-smile. "Glad to see you can get around. Are you hungry?"

"That bacon smells wonderful."

"I thought it might. Do you want eggs and toast with it?"

"Please. Eggs any way you like."

"Can do."

He turned and vanished back into the kitchen. "Coffee?" she heard him call.

"Please. Black."

Apparently she wasn't quite back up to snuff. Realizing she had begun to feel shaky, she made her way back to the sofa and sat. At least now she could sit upright. Last night's ginger ale still sat on the coffee table. It had gone flat, but that didn't keep her from drinking it down in one long draft. Heavens, she was thirsty.

Clint returned just long enough to set a mug of steaming coffee in front of her, then vanished back into the kitchen. He'd added a couple of logs to the fire, and the flames leapt high again, making the room toasty. The fire also cast enough light that she didn't feel any desire to turn on one of the lamps.

It was like being in a warm, cozy cave, she thought. Surrounded by thick walls, safe from predators. But as she'd learned all too painfully, safety was an illusion, one that, in her life, rarely lasted for long.

There was a wooden table with three chairs in one corner of the room, and it was there Clint served their breakfast. He waited for her to get there on her own, watching her as if measuring her steadiness, but not intervening. She didn't want to admit, even to herself, how ready she was to sag into the chair by the time she got there. It wasn't that far, but never before in her life had she felt so weak.

Of course, she hadn't eaten much for days.

Clint apparently believed breakfast should be the day's biggest meal. She found herself looking at platters heaped high with toast, bacon and scrambled eggs.

"That's enough for an army," she remarked in surprise.

"I think you're hungrier than you realize," he responded.

"I think I'm going to prove you right." She was famished, in fact. Except for the cocoa and soda last night, and the crackers and little bit of cinnamon roll, she hadn't eaten in days. Whatever Kevin had intended to do with her, feeding her hadn't been part of it. Three days, she figured. Three days since he'd kidnapped her from Killeen. But that was just a guess, since she'd been stuck in his trunk a lot of the time.

"Want to tell me what happened?" Clint asked.

"Not really." But she knew she would tell him anyway. If the thoughts wouldn't stop running around in her head, where could the harm be in speaking them out loud?

"Eat first," he suggested. "That's the most important thing."

It was. With a shaking hand, she helped herself to healthy portions of eggs, toast and bacon. Hungry though she was, it still seemed difficult to focus on chewing and swallowing. The better she felt, the more the urge to flee grew in her. She had learned that when she held still, danger would find her.

And she could no longer believe it wouldn't find her, regardless of what this man promised.

"So what do you do?" he asked. "For a living."

"Whatever I can. Usually that's waiting tables. It's one of the easiest jobs to get when you're new in a place."

"Do you enjoy it?"

"Mostly. The money is good enough if you work in the right restaurant."

"Do you have any savings?"

"Probably not anymore." Her mood sank again, and she poked at the food on her plate with her fork.

"You know, you should call your bank and tell them your credit card or whatever was stolen on the day you were kidnapped."

"No!" Panic gripped her heart in an icy fist. "Don't you understand? He always finds me somehow. If I poke my head up, they'll want to know where I am. They'll want to know where to send another card. They'll want me to sign things. Once that happens, he'll find me."

He sighed. "You're right, I guess. Sorry, I'm still kind of an electronic Luddite. I keep forgetting that somehow everything is available if you just know how to look for it."

"It seems like it. Almost twenty years ago, the post office stopped giving out forwarding addresses so stalkers couldn't follow people who moved. Maybe that helped back then, but today you can get the address of anyone in the country for a few dollars. And if you have more than a few dollars, apparently you can find out a whole lot more. I'm not sure exactly how he does it, but once I've been in a place for a while, Kevin finds me. Three times now. How the hell do you hide?"

"Actually," he said slowly, "you *can* hide. But it'll involve a lot of changes. We can talk about it later."

She offered to help with the dishes, but he declined, telling her it was better for her to rest. Twenty minutes later, he rejoined her in the living room.

"Do you need to shower?" he asked before he sat. "I can get you some more sweats."

"Maybe later on the shower." She needed one, but she wasn't confident enough of her stability yet, and she sure didn't want to have to ask this stranger for help with *that*.

"Sure. More coffee?"

He freshened her mug and got one of his own before settling into his easy chair. The storm outside kept right on ripping around them. He tilted his head to one side. "This isn't going to blow over soon."

"That's okay," she said. It gave her a few additional hours of safety before she would have to figure out how to move on again.

"I suppose it is."

No, she realized, it *wasn't*. Not for him. He was a self-confessed hermit, and now he was stuck with an invader until such time as he could reasonably boot her out the door.

"I'm sorry," she said.

"For what?"

"Imposing on you like this."

"Oh, for the love of Pete!"

She shrank back against the pillows. He was an unknown, and she hadn't meant to anger him. He could do almost anything to her.

But he remained firmly planted in the chair, though he looked disgusted, a change from his usually unrevealing attitude. "Look," he said, "I know neither of us likes this situation. I prefer my solitude, and you'd sure as hell prefer not to have a lunatic ex-boyfriend trying to kill you, chasing you everywhere you go. But you know what? Sometimes we don't have a choice. We just have to do what needs doing. And right now what needs doing is giving you the safety and space in which to recover. So what if it disturbs my sacred solitude?"

"I'm still sorry," she said, weakly, not sure whether she was sorry for angering him or for the whole damn mess.

"Quit apologizing. You don't have a thing to apologize for. I know I'm not exactly a warm, fuzzy kind of host, but if you think I resent the fact that you need help and I'm here to provide it, you're wrong."

"Okay." She wanted to get away from this topic as quickly as possible.

But even though he could have dropped it there, he didn't. Evidently he had plenty of thoughts on this subject.

"You have rights, and I have responsibilities," he said flatly.

Now, that really did confuse her. "What rights?"

"You," he said, "have a right to exist without terror. You have a right to expect the rest of us to step up and get you away from this guy, since he seems hell-bent on following you wherever you go. You have a right to expect help, and apparently you haven't been getting it."

"But you have rights, too."

"Hell, yeah, but I can protect my own."

"And you don't have a responsibility to me."

"Oh, yeah, I do."

She tried to shake her head, but as soon as she did, she remembered her concussion as pain stabbed her head. "I'm nobody. You don't owe me a thing."

"You're not nobody. You're a human being, and that gives you certain rights in my book. And I'm a human being, and that's enough to make me responsible to do what I can for you."

Her mouth opened a little as she stared at him. She couldn't remember anyone ever putting it like that before.

He leaned forward, putting his mug on the coffee table, then resting his elbows on his knees. "You want to know one of the reasons why I prefer my own company?"

She wasn't sure she did, but he didn't wait for her answer.

"Because too many people have forgotten their responsibilities. Too many people look the other way, or take the easy path. Anything but put themselves out for someone who needs help."

"Not everyone is like that."

"Of course not. But too many are, and I'm sick of them, frankly. All this talk of personal responsibility that people toss around overlooks a very important fact."

"Which is?"

"That your personal responsibility doesn't end at the tip of your own nose. Or at your own front door."

She bit her lip, then ventured, "You've thought a lot about this."

"I spend a lot of time thinking about responsibility. My own. Accepting it. Then deciding what it should have been all along."

She longed to ask him what had put him on such a personal private quest, but didn't dare. There was a darkness in this man that she could feel all the way across the room. It lurked in his gray eyes like a ghost. Maybe it was best not to know.

He picked up his mug again and sat back, sipping slowly while minutes ticked by.

"Any family?" he asked abruptly.

"Me?"

"You."

"No. I oh, do you want to hear the whole story? It sounds like a cliché."

"A lot of life is made up of clichés. Tell me whatever you don't mind sharing."

She looked down and realized her hands were twisting together. She forced herself to separate them and lay them flat. Then she shrugged a shoulder, ignoring the ache. Apparently Kevin had hit her there, too. Not that she remembered, there had been so many blows.

"My mother died of an overdose when I was four. Nobody knew who my dad was. So my grandmother took care of me until she died of a heart attack when I was thirteen. After that it was foster homes. Six of them. I don't think I was easy to deal with. And there's nobody else."

"You made it through high school, though?"

"Yeah. Yeah, I did. I always wanted to go to college, but I had to take care of myself and kept putting it off and then…well, Kevin…" She bit her lip again, unable to meet his gaze.

"Tell me about Kevin. About the beginning."

She hesitated, unable to imagine why he wanted all this information, but reluctant to tell him it was none of his business. He'd rescued her in the middle of a blizzard where she probably would have died except for him. That gave him a right to know, she supposed. Especially since he was still helping her.

"Kevin was okay at first. Really nice. It was a long time before I realized that I was tiptoeing around all the time because of his temper. It took me even longer to realize he couldn't hold a job for more than a month or two, and finally I gave up even trying to tell him to look for work. So I did something stupid."

"And that was?"

She drew a long breath. "I started skimming my paycheck."

"You what?" He sounded utterly disbelieving. "How can you skim your own paycheck?"

"I got a raise and didn't tell him. I'd go to the bank and split the deposit, put the extra money into a savings account. I meant to save for school."

"And you didn't tell him."

"No."

He sighed. "That's a warning sign in huge red letters. But I suppose he had you so intimidated by that point that you didn't even recognize it."

"Not really. I just did it. I didn't exactly think about all the reasons I felt the need to. When I look back, I feel stupid."

"No, don't. You have no idea how many people, doing the best they can in whatever situation they're in, look back later and think they were stupid. It's never stupid. It's the best you can do at the time."

"Thanks. I still feel stupid."

"So let me guess. He found out about the savings account."

She nodded. "That was the first time he beat me."

"And then he was oh so apologetic, swore he'd never do it again and took the money."

"Yeah. Like I said, stupid."

"Stop saying that. It's amazing how manipulative these bastards can be. It's like they're born knowing how to get what they want. So okay, that was the first time the line got crossed. And it got worse, right?"

"Yeah. With time. Until finally he broke my arm and left my face such a mess I couldn't go to work, and my boss actually came to the house. He took one look at me and dragged me to the hospital, then called the cops."

"Ah, a responsible person arrives on the scene. Amazing."

In spite of herself, she felt the unbruised side of her face lift in a slight smile. "My boss was a good man."

"I agree. So Kevin went to jail?"

"That time."

"But he got out."

"Of course. Less than two years later."

"I think I can pretty much write the rest of the story." He sipped his coffee and closed his eyes for a moment. When they opened, they held an ice that should have frightened her, but somehow it didn't. Maybe she was too tired, too battered. Maybe she just couldn't rustle up any more terror.

"Take my word for it, Kay Young, as long as you are in this house, that man will not lay a finger on you."

Deep inside she shivered, because she believed him, because she feared the kind of protection he was capable of providing. Special Ops? Yeah, he could protect her.

"I don't want you to get into any trouble on my account," she blurted.

He smiled, but not pleasantly.

"I won't," he said. "Trust me, I won't."

She dozed off again, and when she woke, she felt disoriented. Not because she didn't recognize the cabin or the fireplace, or Clint sitting across the way in his chair reading. No, it was something even more basic than that.

Almost before she opened her eyes, she asked, "What time is it? What day is it?"

He looked up from his book. "It's Friday, December twelfth and it's just after one in the afternoon."

"Five days!"

"Since he took you?"

"Yes." She looked around, trying to center herself somehow. "What state did you say this was?"

"Wyoming. Conard County, Wyoming, to be more precise."

She squeezed her eyes shut. "Sorry. It's like things are jumbled."

"That's normal enough, I suppose. How's your head feel?"

"The headache is almost gone."

"Good. That's probably why you're trying to sort things out."

"I didn't know he had me so long."

"No?"

"No. He kept me in the trunk a lot. He didn't feed me. He hardly gave me any water."

"He would be wise not to come near you while I'm around."

She looked at him, amazed by the calm way he spoke, as if such threats were commonplace in his world. Not a ripple of emotion showed on his face. Oddly, while his obvious self-control was horrifying in a way, it also reassured her far more than a display of anger would have. Far more.

Outside, judging from the sound of the wind, the storm still raged. Hard to believe it had gone on so long. Hard to accept that she was trapped in more ways than one.

"I've got to figure out what to do."

"Relax," he said. "I'm already figuring it out."

"Why should *you* do that?"

He shrugged. "Why not?"

"Because it's *my* problem?"

"It's mine now, too."

She realized he meant it. That was no token statement. "I can figure it out."

"You've been figuring it out for a few years now. Let somebody else help you for a change." He closed his book and placed it on the coffee table. "I'm not trying to take over, it's not my place. You can make all the decisions yourself. But I have a few suggestions."

"Like what?"

"For starters, we call the sheriff."

"No! Then I'll be in the blotter. I'll be in the newspaper, like last time I made a complaint. I don't want him to know I'm still in the area!"

He waited a moment before speaking. When he did, his voice was so calm it seemed at odds with the situation. "Are you planning to run forever?"

She bit her lip so hard it hurt. "No," she said finally, feeling her eyes sting. "No."

"Then we need to deal with the problem. The sheriff here is a man I'd trust with my life, and I don't say that about many people. If I tell him what's going on, he'll guard your secret with his life. Your name won't be in any blotter or any report."

"You're sure?"

"Like I said, I'd trust him with my life. In fact, there are a few people hereabouts I can say that about. So trust me on this one."

"And if I do?"

"Then we're going to ask the sheriff to find Kevin. Find him and nail him good. It's not just beating you up anymore, Kay. It's kidnapping. Across state lines. That's a federal crime, and that son of a bitch is going away for life."

A spark of hope ignited in her, but then flickered out. "He has to be caught first."

"Trust me, we'll get him. One way or another."

"But it's just my word against his." That hadn't been enough before.

"Well, I think some photos of your face will make a point. And the other injuries he gave you."

She touched her cheek lightly with her fingertips. "I must look awful."

"You look like someone who was hit in the side of the head with something heavy. Like a tire iron."

She almost gasped. "How did you know?"

"Did you look in the mirror when you went to the bathroom?"

"No." No, she had avoided that like the plague. It was bad enough to endure the pain, but she'd been afraid to look for fear he'd ruined her face for good. How could she work as a waitress with a messed-up face?

"If we can't get the sheriff out here soon, I'm going to ask you to let me take some pictures myself."

"Why do we have to wait for the sheriff?"

"I think it's more evidentiary if he does it. Well, actually, he'll probably ask one of his female deputies to do it. From what I saw when I helped you change into those clothes yesterday, you were beaten all over."

She covered her face with her hands, pierced by a shame she couldn't explain. Why should she feel shame? But she did, and it was deep and burning. She felt hot tears begin to run, but no sobs accompanied them. She'd learned, a long time ago, to cry silently.

At least her stranger-savior didn't evince any annoyance. He just let her cry. Later, when the tears dried and she dabbed at her face with the sleeves of the green sweatshirt, he rose, returning a minute later with a box of tissues and a fresh cup of coffee.

She took the tissues gratefully, dabbing her face, blowing her nose. "Sorry," she said.

"No need."

The coffee tasted as if it had been freshly brewed, and she sipped it with pleasure. She hadn't really tasted anything before, had just been going through the motions, but now, for the first time in days, she discovered she could savor something simple. Something good. "You like it strong. So do I." She gave him a smile with the half of her face that still felt mobile.

He acknowledged her words with a small nod. Evidently he didn't run to social pleasantries.

"When are you going to call the sheriff?"

"As soon as you're ready to give me identifying information."

"What kind of information?"

"The car he was driving, what he looks like, his full name, where he kidnapped you from."

"Okay." She drew a deep breath. He was right; she couldn't keep running. And this was as good a place as any to make her stand, if only because she seemed to have an ally.

An odd ally, one who apparently had chosen to stand beside her on principle and nothing else. But maybe that was the best kind of ally—one who expected nothing from her but merely felt her situation deserved his help.

Yes, that was best, she decided. That way there was no chance of the kind of messiness she'd run into with Kevin.

"I'll give you whatever information you want."

He nodded again and rose. "Just let me get a pad and pen."

She waited, holding her mug in both hands, afraid to nurture even a spark of hope. For all she knew, she was about to sign her own death warrant.

But even death seemed preferable to living like this any longer.

Chapter 4

Clint got his cordless phone and returned to his easy chair, putting the pad on his lap. Kay had answered his questions, and he'd scribbled down the answers. It was time to call the sheriff, Gage Dalton, even though the roads for miles around were impassable.

He didn't need the sheriff to protect Kay here at his house. He needed the sheriff to keep eyes out for Kevin.

He scanned the pad to refresh his memory of what she had told him before he dialed. His notes were even more abbreviated than his speech, but he had a good memory.

A memory that was suddenly jogged as he scanned the description of the car.

God! Reaching back to the moments when he had been carrying Kay to his truck, he remembered a car passing them and slowing down. He couldn't be sure it exactly matched her description, because by then they'd been approaching whiteout conditions, but it came close enough to give him a minor adrenaline jolt.

If that had been Kevin, then there was now a chance he had a pretty good idea where Kay was. Because the road dead-ended, he would have had to backtrack, and he would have at least an idea that Clint had taken her to his ranch. And worse, if he'd scanned the license tag, it would be easy enough to find out exactly where Clint lived. So if Kevin checked around and found that Kay hadn't gone to the police or into the hospital, he would be virtually certain that she was still with Clint.

In this storm he would be as immobilized as everyone else, but after the roads were cleared…

A thrum of anger started beating in time with his heart. He didn't say anything to Kay, though. She was already skittish enough. So skittish he wanted her to hear every word he spoke to the sheriff so she would know he hadn't betrayed her in any way.

But even as he punched in the non-emergency number, his mind was beginning to turn over plans for making his cabin safer.

"Conard County Sheriff's Office," said the froggy voice of the dispatcher. Rain or shine, blizzard or forest fire, Velma was always at the other end of the line.

"Hi, Velma, this is Clint Ardmore. I need to talk to Gage."

"Well, honey, I'll see what I can do, but as you can imagine, we're trying to help folks who got themselves into a passel of trouble by not staying home in this crud."

"Sounds to me like you didn't stay home, either."

Velma laughed, a sound similar to a braying donkey. "Honey, I only have to *walk* a couple of blocks. Gage is out somewhere with a crew, trying to pull a family out of a ditch. Say... Micah's not too far from you. Want me to have him drop by?"

Micah Parish was another of the handful of local people that Clint would have trusted with his life. But he looked over at Kay and wondered if she would be able to take it. She was twisting her hands again, and biting her lip, looking ready to jump out of her skin.

On the other hand, now that he'd recalled that car, he couldn't forget it.

"How," he asked Velma, "can Micah get here?"

"He's plowing his way in. You're on the route." All the deputies had plows on the fronts of their official vehicles exactly for times like this.

"Give me a sec, Velma."

"Sure."

He put his hand over the mouthpiece. "Kay? One of those guys I'd trust my life to?"

"Yes?"

"He's going to be driving past here. Talking to him would be better than waiting for the sheriff. Apparently he's pretty tied up with people who have storm trouble."

Her hands tightened around each other until her knuckles turned white. "You're sure?" she finally asked hesitantly.

"Well, if he comes here, you can make sure he doesn't write anything down. Maybe that would make you feel better. And I can't think of a better person to have my back."

Finally she nodded. "Okay. Okay." But she didn't sound happy.

He took his hand from the mouthpiece. "Velma? Yeah, that would be great if Micah would stop by. I really need to talk to him."

"Consider it done. I'll call him now."

"Thanks."

When he disconnected, Clint put the handset on the table beside him. "It'll be okay," he said, feeling once again as if he was trying to calm a frightened horse. He'd calmed frightened men in battle, but this was a whole different thing, calling for a different kind of patience, a kind he wasn't sure he had enough of.

He ran through an assortment of cuss words in his head, because he was sure if he said any of them aloud she would shrink away again, and as much as he had tried to harden himself over the years, seeing a woman shrink from him brought back enough memories to fill a dump truck and make him feel like an utter bastard.

The phone rang. It was Velma. "Micah is plowing his way up your road right now. He said to thank you for those reflector posts you put up last year."

Clint gave a rare chuckle. He'd lined his driveway with the things after a blizzard almost as bad as this one, because his drive was long enough, and winding enough, to be impossible to find under heavy snow, and even more impossible to clear. "Tell him thanks for clearing the road for me."

"You'll just have to clear it again later," Velma advised him. "The snow is going to stop soon, but the wind will keep up until tomorrow. Like holding a flood back with a broom." On that positive note, she disconnected.

Clint looked at Kay again. She appeared to have sunk into unhappy recollection. "Micah will be here soon. He's plowing his way to the door."

He watched her eyes widen and fill with fear, and then gave her points for quickly getting a grip on her emotions. "Okay," she said on a tight breath.

Nothing he could tell her would reassure her. She was running on an awful lot of trust right now, and as someone who'd learned to trust very few, he could understand that.

Micah arrived fifteen minutes later. They could hear the engine strain as he approached, pushing heavy snow out of the way. Then he left the vehicle idling. They heard the stomp of boots on the porch as he shook the snow off, and at the sound, Kay shrank visibly.

Clint stifled a sigh and went to get the door, letting Micah in with a cold blast of air and swirling snow. Micah was every bit as big as Clint, broad and well-muscled, but far more exotic looking thanks to his Cherokee heritage.

Clint had to force the door closed against the wind, then latched it firmly.

"Damn," Micah said. "Somebody moved Antarctica up here."

"It's bad," Clint agreed as they shook hands. "Coffee?

"Hot and black."

But something else had to come first. "Come meet my guest."

Micah's black-as-night eyes slipped past him and found Kay, who sat up and was looking at him with evident terror.

"Well, hell," Micah said. "Who the devil beat her up?"

* * *

Kay sat on the very edge of the couch, poised to run even though there was nowhere she could flee. Another man, another dangerous man, this one older but every bit as huge as Clint. She felt like a mouse facing two lions.

"Kay," Clint said, "this is Deputy Micah Parish. Micah, Kay Young."

"Howdy," Micah said. Then he pulled off his jacket, revealing a tan deputy's uniform and badge. He hung the coat on the peg by the door. "First the coffee. Then the talk. I've been on the road for three hours now, and the heater in the damn truck is barely working. Too much wind, I think. Engine's not getting very warm."

"Take a seat. I'll be right back. Kay, you want more coffee?"

She managed a slight negative shake of her head as she tried to cope with the fact that after running from a man for three years, she was now dependent on two of them, both of them looking as if they could do a lot more damage with their bare hands than Kevin could do with a tire iron.

Micah stepped farther into the room and settled on the one remaining chair. He seemed to know that the easy chair was Clint's preferred perch. He held his hands out to the fire for a minute, then turned toward her slowly. She shrank back.

"Easy, girl," he said quietly. "Nobody here is gonna hurt you."

She didn't exactly have any choice now except to believe him. Cold comfort.

Clint returned with two mugs and passed one to Micah.

"Thanks," Micah said, as Clint settled into his chair. "So is this what it looks like?"

"Maybe. But maybe worse."

Micah sipped his hot coffee, then returned his dark gaze to Kay.

What were they talking about? Her? She wished she could hide behind the sofa pillows. And yet she sensed no threat in those exotic eyes.

"My wife," Micah said.

She managed a slight nod.

"My wife was on the run from an abusive ex-husband when I found her. There was a storm, not as bad as this, but still a storm. She was driving too fast, so I pulled her over to warn her to slow down. I got to know her terror pretty quick."

Something inside Kay seemed to pop. Maybe the bubble of fear and apprehension. She relaxed a bit. "Did he follow her?"

"Yeah, he did."

"Where is he now?"

"Well, he tried to kill her. So I had to kill him."

She sagged then, as the last of the tension seeped out of her. She looked at Clint and realized he was prepared to do the same if necessary. Oh, Lord, she didn't want anybody to die, but she was beginning to think there was no other way out.

Clint spoke. "He kidnapped Kay from Texas and got her this far before she managed to escape."

"Kidnapping is good," Micah remarked. "Especially across state lines."

"It is?" Kay could scarcely believe she had heard right, and fear began to trickle along her spine.

"It's very good," Micah said. "The Feds can usually get a maximum sentence on a case like that."

"I'd like that," Kay admitted, trying to relax again. "I'm so tired of running." Her chest tightened, and she had to fight back tears. Tired. Yes she was tired. Tired to the very bone. At last she felt secure enough to settle back more comfortably on the sofa.

Micah nodded and then turned back to Clint. "So tell me what you have."

"First, Kay doesn't want her name on any records. Not until you catch the guy."

"I can do that."

Kay released another relieved sigh and let her eyes close for a minute. Thank God. She listened as Clint related the information she'd given him, Kevin's name, age, even his social security number, and the description of the car. And then the description of her abduction and mistreatment. Brief though the account was, she found it painful to listen to. And even though she had been the victim, she could hardly believe it. It sounded so different coming out of Clint's mouth.

Micah took the pad from Clint and turned to a fresh sheet. "Some of this can go in the record. I'll need it to put out a BOLO." But even as he started to write, he paused and looked at Kay. "Not your name. We don't need *your* name now, okay? Nor do I need to tell anyone where you are. But he already knows you escaped in these parts so that won't tell him anything he doesn't know."

"Thank you."

Micah finished writing down the information, then ripped the sheet off the pad. "I can get this out right away. I'm going out to the car to get my camera, so I can take some pictures of you. You probably won't want me to see everything, but the fresher the photos are, the better, and my camera is time and date stamped. It's evidence, all right?"

She nodded, compressing her lips. "Okay." This was going to be so humiliating. Somehow, displaying her wounds seemed like an admission of her own failures.

Micah's face gentled. "If I could get a female deputy out here, I would. Maybe after the wind dies down. But right now it's just me, and we don't need lawyers arguing about whether those bruises were too old to have occurred during the kidnapping."

She hadn't thought about that, but she could see his point. From somewhere she found a bit of resolve. "Okay," she said again. If she had to face Kevin down in a courtroom again, she didn't want to be accused of lying, like last time. Or, if she *was* accused of it, she wanted proof that she wasn't.

She put her hand to her head as Micah rose and went to get his camera.

"Headache?" Clint asked immediately.

"No. I don't know. I just can't seem to get my footing. It's like things are changing so fast."

"When we've been through a really bad time, it's harder to adjust to changes for a while."

"Maybe." But it was even harder to let go of her fear. "I don't really know how to relax anymore," she blurted with sudden realization.

"I know that feeling all too well. It takes time, a lot of time, to realize you can climb down from the ceiling safely."

She supposed he would know. But then Micah came back in with the camera, and she faced more humiliation. However, he didn't ask for much. He squatted right in front of her.

"I'm going to take pictures of your face," he said gently. "Just your face. If it's hard to move, say so, and I'll do all the moving."

"I think I can do it."

He started snapping. The flash was on, of course, which made her keep blinking, but since this wasn't a fashion shoot, she didn't think it mattered. He must have taken a dozen photos of her face from different angles before he said, "Anything else you feel comfortable showing me?"

"Her back," Clint said.

She started to protest, but he spoke first. "Kay, we can get your back without offending your modesty. I'll help."

So she stood up, away from the furniture, and let Clint pull up the back of the sweatshirt until her entire back and shoulders were revealed while she clutched the front securely to her breasts.

"Well, hell," Micah said again, and the flashes started. "Any more like that?"

"All over her," Clint said. "But I think you've got the worst ones." He let the sweatshirt fall back into place.

"Make a note of the others," Micah suggested. "I'll get Sara out here tomorrow, assuming we've finished rescuing fools."

Kay made her way back to the couch and sat, resting her face in her hands again, at least as much as she could without making it hurt worse. Not that she didn't hurt all over, but the wound to her face seemed to dominate her awareness much more than her back or the rest of her.

Micah stayed only a few more minutes, then remarked that he had to get on to other things. Kay noticed that Clint followed him out onto the porch, brutal as the weather was, and the two men stood talking for a couple of minutes.

But she was past caring what they might be discussing. Fatigue was washing over her in waves again, and she didn't have the energy to fight it. She reached for the quilt, moving gingerly, and pulled it up over herself as she tried to burrow into the couch as if it were a private cave.

Enough, she thought. Enough.

Silent tears spilled down her face, but she hardly noticed them as she hid from the world and quickly slipped into sleep. Sleep, it seemed, was her last refuge.

Outside, Clint had more important matters on his mind. "I think this Kevin guy may have seen me pick her up along the road. A car came by as I was carrying her to my truck, and it slowed down. I thought at the time it was someone heading up to the Rivers place, but when she gave me the description of the car, I started to wonder. I didn't take all that good a look. We were getting into whiteout conditions."

Micah rocked a bit on his heels. Snow whirled like tiny tornadoes just beyond the porch, and some of it blew into their faces, stinging. "Not good. You want someone out here?"

"You can't spare anybody right now. Besides, I can keep her safe in the house."

"Yeah." Micah rubbed his chin. "That sumbitch probably won't be trying to get around in this weather anyway. All right, I'll get everyone on alert. If we're lucky, he's stuck in a snowbank somewhere."

"We can hope." But Clint wasn't the hopeful type. He'd had too much experience with Murphy's law. He always prepared for the worst.

"Do you have everything you need? Food? Fuel?"

"Do you need to ask?"

Micah chuckled. "No, I guess not. We come from the same school." He started to step off the porch, then looked back. "You know, I could take her to my place."

Clint knew exactly what he meant. Micah understood his need for solitude, at one time had even shared it.

"No," he said. "No. I took this one on, and I'm not pushing it off on anybody else. Besides, it could put your family at risk, and you can't be there round the clock."

Micah gave a nod of acknowledgment, then waded through the snow to his truck. With a wave, he headed out.

Clint stood outside in the biting wind and snow awhile longer, listening to the fading sound of the deputy's engine. The wind was fast filling in the gap left by the plow.

The world could be such a sorry place. Enough to make a man feel ashamed of being human. But not always. He might find his comfort in the basic innocence of nature. What could be purer than a world covered in fresh snow? But even as he looked out into the wrath of nature, he knew life-and-death struggles were going on all around him. The difference was most of those struggles weren't about power, just survival.

So what did that leave a man? Atonement. Basic atonement.

And a small part of his atonement was waiting right inside his living room.

Chapter 5

Kay awoke from a miserable sleep in which both the pains in her body and nightmares had disturbed her. As her eyes opened, she was surprised to see a propane lantern on the coffee table, providing the only light in the room except for the fireplace.

Away from the light, in the darker corners, the firelight made shadows dance and flicker. She turned her head and saw Clint in his easy chair, a shadowed figure himself.

"The power went out," he said when he saw her wake.

Since she could still hear the wind keening like a banshee, she had a pretty good idea why. "Oh." She struggled with the quilt she had managed to tangle all around herself until she could sit up a little higher.

"Need anything?" he asked. "We're pretty much okay, except we won't have running water until the power comes back on. I've got enough stashed for drinking and cooking, but I can't offer that shower right now."

"That's okay." What else could she say? It was only now, anyway, as her injuries began to mend, that she noticed how grimy she felt. Still, she could stand another few hours.

"I was thinking, though, that if we don't get power back soon, I can heat up some water and make you a bath. A small bath, but I can do it."

"That's kind of you, but maybe we better save the water." She was touched by his caring.

"Well, I don't imagine you got the chance to clean up during your abduction and I know how important that can be psychologically."

She tried to smile, but mostly she was surprised by how much he seemed to understand. Understanding had been lacking in a lot of her life. For the first time since he had found her, she felt a flicker of real warmth toward him.

He stood. "Do you need something to drink?"

"I'm fine right now."

"Okay. I'm going to go out and walk around a bit, make sure the wind isn't doing any damage. Shouldn't take me long."

She nodded, but her instant response wasn't exactly positive. Logically it made sense that he would want to look for wind damage, but emotionally she felt terrified that he might really be looking for something—some*one*—else.

Stop it, she told herself. There was no reason on earth to think that Kevin could possibly know she was here, or that Clint would be worried about it.

But long conditioning refused to let her relax. Fear seemed to have engraved itself on her very being.

She listened as he pulled on his outerwear to go out and face the furious elements. Then the door slammed and she was alone, and for the first time in a very long time, being alone didn't feel safe.

God, she was a mess. And getting messier by the moment, it seemed. After living in survival mode, always looking over her shoulder, it seemed that even the hint of safety had shattered her coping mechanisms.

She couldn't help it. She sat up completely, putting her feet on the floor, then waited tensely. Kevin had stripped her of her last sense of security, even self-deluded security.

She tried to think about Clint instead. An enigma, she decided, with a pockmarked soul. Good at heart, but damaged. Badly damaged. Like her. God knew what wounds *he* carried, and he didn't seem likely to tell her.

But even in the midst of her own selfish fear, she could feel a twinge of genuine sympathy for him. Just from occasional things he'd said, she suspected that he'd put himself in his hermitage less from general disgust with people than from disgust from himself.

But maybe she was reading too much into things. Maybe he'd meant exactly what he'd said about being fed up with selfish people. Even if that were true, she didn't believe that was the sum of it. The man had a side he kept showing in spite of himself, a generous side enhanced by a strong sense of duty.

And he was protective. Imagine him understanding her unwillingness to expose her wounds to Micah. Almost as if he understood that they were more than just external bruises but a mark of her shame. And then his thoughtfulness in the way he had helped preserve her modesty while revealing her back and shoulders to the camera.

No, he might be trying to turn into stone. He might think he'd looked into the face of Medusa and was now just rock. But that wasn't true. Not at all. No one with a heart of stone would have cared for her the way he had.

She almost gasped when he came back in. Instinct made her turn sharply toward the door, to be sure it was him, and she almost groaned as she rediscovered all her bruises. "Oh God," she whispered as the wave of agony passed through her.

He never paused to drop his jacket or kick off his boots. He came shooting over to her like a bullet and squatted in front of her. "What's wrong?"

She had to struggle to get her breath back. Each time she inhaled, it hurt again. "I just moved wrong," she gasped finally. "I think my ribs may be bruised."

"I wouldn't be surprised. How bad does it hurt?"

"It's going away."

"You're really going to have to consider seeing a doctor as soon as we can get out of here."

"I'll be *fine*." She sounded angry, but she was actually terrified by the thought. If she saw a doctor, another person would know she was here. And how the hell would she pay for it, anyway?

He remained squatting in front of her as snow began to melt off his jacket and boots. "Okay," he said finally.

"Okay?"

He gave her a crooked smile. "There's no point in having this fight right now, when all I could do is get us stuck in the snow."

"Oh." In spite of herself, one corner of her mouth lifted. "Yeah, it would be stupid to argue now."

"We'll revisit this in the morning." He rose and went to remove his outerwear by the door. Then he fetched a ragged towel and mopped the small puddles he'd left on the floor.

"How is it out there?" she asked, desperate for the distraction. Breathing was getting easier, and slowly she sank back against the pillows.

"Frankly? Awful. It may have stopped snowing, but you couldn't prove it by me. The wind is a killer. It's a good day for staying in your lair and sitting by the fire."

"Sounds like it." And but for him, she would be lying under a snow blanket, probably until spring, when someone found her and named her Jane Doe. She squeezed her eyes closed for a minute, seeking some kind of balance internally. No point in thinking like that. It hadn't happened. Instead, she was warm and safe.

For now.

"Pain?" he asked.

She opened her eyes and found him in his chair again. "No, not really. Just wrestling with demons."

"Sometimes it helps to call a time-out."

"I'm still trying to find a way to do that."

"It can take a while." He drummed his fingers briefly on the arm of his chair. "I'm not much of a distraction," he finally said. "I don't talk much. Hell, I even quit playing poker, not that it's much fun with only two players."

"Trust me, I'm not complaining. You've done more for me than most people ever have."

He shook his head. "I've done very little. Don't build me up into something I'm not."

Surprise washed away her other thoughts. Could he really feel that way? Even cops who were supposed to protect her had done less than this man, especially when measured against his obvious preference for solitude. "I think you underrate yourself."

"No, I've just taken a good hard look at myself."

"But…" She stopped. Arguing about the kind of man he was wouldn't help anything at all. It might even anger him. And he certainly wouldn't listen to her, because she didn't really know him. "I'm grateful to you. Very grateful."

"Probably," he acknowledged. "And probably more than I deserve. Are you getting hungry?"

She recognized the quick change in subject as a warning and let it lie. He didn't think he deserved her gratitude. God, talk about a pair of wounded souls!

"I run by my internal clock these days," he went on, "and I could use a sandwich. Tuna sound good?"

"It sounds great."

He was up and out of that chair as if he'd just been released from Old Sparky.

She watched his back as he walked toward the kitchen and felt a quiver of interest in him as a man, the first sexual impulse she'd felt since Kevin had beaten her the first time.

No, she warned herself. Don't let that happen. No men. Ever again. And certainly not one who preferred living alone. That was borrowing trouble, and she already had enough of that on her tail.

But apparently there was a part of her that hadn't died in the assaults of the last three years, a part that still wanted to believe in happily-ever-after and a man who could make her feel good things again.

Stupid. All a bunch of myths, as well she ought to know. In the end, she could rely on no one but herself for her happiness and safety.

But sometimes logic was a cold companion, and the heart refused to be silenced. Her dreams might lie shattered around her, but they still had some life.

The question, really, was whether it was worth trying to put them back together again.

No, she decided. It would be too dangerous. Far too dangerous to ever risk herself again.

Clint returned with a couple of plates and napkins. He placed one plate on the coffee table in front of her, the other beside his chair. He disappeared for a minute into the kitchen again and returned with two glasses of ginger ale.

"Thank you," Kay said.

"Eat up, and if you want more, there's plenty."

Tuna on rye. A lot of tuna. She doubted she would be able to eat all of one sandwich, let alone another. "Oh, this is good," she said after she had savored a bite.

He gave her his almost-smile. "I eat a lot of tuna. If I didn't make it well, I would be an unhappy, hungry man."

A little laugh escaped her, a small one in deference to her bruised ribs. "What's that about necessity?"

"The mother of all invention."

"Yeah."

His smile deepened a shade. "You're going to be all right, you know."

She paused, a mix of feelings flooding her. "How can you know that?"

"Because you've got spunk."

That warmed her. She wasn't sure he was right, but the compliment warmed her anyway. What had she done, after all, except what she'd *had* to do? She sipped her ginger ale and took another bite of her sandwich.

"So what do you do?" she asked him.

"I'm a writer."

"What kind?"

He shrugged. "I do some action-adventure novels, mostly for fun. It's a way to pay bills. Then I write other stuff."

"What kind of stuff?"

He hesitated. "I write a lot about ethics."

"Really?" That piqued her attention. "Do you mean papers or articles or what?"

"I've written a number of journal articles, and one book on what they call 'Just War Theory.' Basically, discussing what situations can justify fighting a war."

She forgot her sandwich and looked at him with amazement. "I thought only professors did that kind of stuff."

"Well, a few of us out here don't teach, we just think too much."

It sounded almost like he was joking, but she couldn't be sure. "I wasn't putting you down, I'm just kind of amazed."

"Yeah, me and Thoreau. Backwoods philosophers."

"But you must need a lot of education to get to the point where you can write journal articles the way you do."

"Over the years, when I was in the military, I took a lot of classes. Somehow they eventually added up to a PhD."

"Oh, wow." She stared at him, impressed.

He waved a dismissive hand. "No biggie. The military pushes education. They make it easy to take classes."

"But you went all the way."

He shook his head. "It was an escape."

She longed to ask how that could be. "Maybe I'll get to college eventually."

He nodded. "I believe you will."

She wished she could be as certain.

"Any idea what you'd like to study?"

She shook her head. "Not yet. I've thought about things like being a nurse, but I don't know if I could pass all the classes."

"Well, college is great, especially the first couple of years. They give you an opportunity to try on all kinds of things for size. You'll find what you like."

"I hope so. I don't mind waiting tables at all, but I have so many questions about things. And as time passes, I seem to get more curious."

"Curiosity is good."

"So this book you wrote—*Just War Theory*? What is that?"

"It's a lot of philosophical thinking about what can morally justify war. People have been asking and trying to answer that question for a long time. People with consciences, anyway."

"And your book?"

"Well, I did the usual overview, then put my own spin on some of it."

She sensed she wouldn't be able to understand if she pressed him any further. "I hope someday I'll know enough so I can read it."

"It's dry, unless that's your thing."

"Was it successful?"

"That depends on what you mean by success. It didn't make me rich. But it's being used in a number of colleges and universities."

"That's success."

"Getting read is success."

She smiled and reached for her sandwich again. "I guess so. Being ignored would be awful."

"In this business, it would be a death knell. Much better to annoy people."

"Really? Why?"

"Because it stimulates discussion. Nothing makes me happier than when my e-mail box gets full because a new semester has begun and a bunch of people want to argue with me."

"I honestly can't imagine that. I think it would intimidate me."

"It makes me rub my hands with glee."

She laughed, then winced. "I don't think that's me."

"Maybe not. We're all different."

And he was definitely a puzzle. A hermit who liked to argue with people. By e-mail. So he hadn't totally cut himself off, he'd just set up barriers. High ones, evidently, ones that guarded him from everything except intellectual interaction.

She could understand that. It would be nice if her world would resolve into that kind of neatness.

But not *exactly* that kind of neatness. She didn't think she was built to live alone and intellectualize things.

Before Kevin, she'd always had a large circle of friends she liked spending time with. After Kevin, that first time, when she had thought she was safe again, she'd rebuilt her circle.

Then she had learned to avoid connections, because every time Kevin found her again, she had to give them up. It was painful to have to run again, but even more so if she had to leave behind people she cared about.

She invested nothing of herself in life anymore, nothing beyond trying to get by. So how was she different from Clint?

She lost her taste for the sandwich and slipped the plate back onto the table, wincing as she did so.

"Full?" he asked.

"Full enough." Full enough of *everything,* including her own misery.

"You know," he said slowly, "I can heat up that water and you could soak a bit. It might help with the aches and pains."

"But I don't want to waste your water. We don't know how long this might go on."

He shrugged. "If worse comes to worse, I can melt plenty of snow in front of the fire. It's not like we're in the middle of the desert."

She had to smile at that. "I guess not."

"So let me make you a bath. You need to soak out some of the soreness."

She had to admit that sounded good. "If you wouldn't mind?"

"Lady, I'd rather be busy any day than staring at the walls. I can't even work right now with the power out."

"Then I'd love a bath."

"Consider it done as soon as I'm through eating."

"Thank you."

He was as good as his word. Astonishment took her when she saw the number of huge pots he had. "Do you cook for an army or something?"

"You can never have too many pots for an emergency. I wouldn't cook in these, they're too thin, but they're great for boiling water."

Which he managed to do in surprisingly short order by using both the propane stove and the fireplace. When he at last called her to the bathroom, steam was rising from the tub. A couple of candles burned on the rim, safely out of the way, shedding extra light to compensate for the thin gray daylight that came through the single window.

"It's too hot, obviously, but I'm going to add cold water now. You tell me when the temperature's right."

So she sat on the toilet beside the tub while he added cold water, then stuck her finger in to test. Finally she said, "It's probably just about right now."

"Okay. I'll leave it there, then. I'll keep another pot on the stove in case you want a reheat." He paused. "By the way, if you want more hot water, don't be too modest to ask. I can walk in here backward."

He also brought her a fresh set of sweats, blue this time, and a couple of clean towels. Then he set a bottle on the edge of the tub. "Shampoo, if you want it. I don't have any of those fancy bath salts, though. Sorry."

She was touched that he would even think of such a thing. "I don't use them anyway."

"If you need anything at all, just call me."

Her first thought as he closed the door behind him was that she hoped she didn't have to call him for anything. Then she remembered that he had redressed her after finding her. It wasn't like she had anything he hadn't already seen, even if she didn't remember the moment.

Moving gingerly, she shed the sweats she wore, steadied herself with a hand on the side of the tub and eased into the water. It was actually a bit too hot, but she didn't care. She would get used to it quickly enough, and the hope of easing some of her aches overrode everything else, even the desire to be clean again.

She didn't even try to move once she had settled into the water. It rose to her neck if she sank just a little, and she laid her head back against a towel, closed her eyes and let the heat do its work. God, it was heaven.

When was the last time she'd felt safe enough to indulge in such a luxury? She couldn't remember. For a long time now she'd taken showers, hurrying through them. Five minutes max, because she couldn't forget how vulnerable she was when bathing. That was another legacy of Kevin. When you never knew when you were going to need to run, you didn't let yourself get into a situation where you couldn't get away quickly.

Her eyes flew open as ice rattled against the frosted glass window over the tub. Nothing out there. Nothing. She was safe, she reminded herself. Clint was just outside that door, near enough to hear a single cry. Nasty as Kevin could be, she doubted he could stand up for long to Clint. Nor could he get her very far in this storm.

No, she was safe. She willed her body to recognize that and relax again. It would have been so nice to nod off right now, but an acute awareness of her nakedness, and thus her vulnerability, wouldn't allow her.

She wondered if she would ever get past this constant insecurity and fear. Maybe, if Kevin went to prison for twenty years, then after a few years she could relax again.

But that kind of security was something she could only dream of now; it was nothing she could really believe in. Not yet.

There was a knock on the door, and she started, realizing the bath had begun to go cold. She must have nodded off right in the middle of thinking about her own fear.

"Kay? Are you all right?"

"I guess I fell asleep."

"That's good. Need more hot water?"

She considered it. "No, thanks. I'm just going to wash fast and get out of here." Because the fears that lurked in the corners of her mind were trying to bite again, insisting that she remember she was *never* safe. Not even now.

"Okay. Holler if you need help."

The heat had done its job, though, and she found it easy enough to wash herself with a bar of soap and a washcloth. Then she submerged her head to wet her hair and stifled groans as she shampooed. She was feeling better, yes, but not perfect.

Finally she submerged her head one more time and ran her fingers through her hair, working the shampoo out.

No, not perfect, but much better. With a toe, she pulled the plug and let the water start to drain.

She was feeling a whole lot better by the time she reached for the side of the tub and realized she couldn't get out.

Getting in had been a lot easier than trying to lever herself up. Dammit! Her arms and sides screamed at the effort of trying to lift herself. Now what?

She tried again, but the pain only got worse. And now she was shaking and getting cold. Oh, this wasn't fair!

But what the hell was fair in life? Not a damn thing.

She gave it one more try, and a cry escaped her as her muscles and ribs rebelled.

"Kay? *Kay?*"

She pressed her forehead to the edge of the tub, mad at her own helplessness, embarrassed beyond belief, ashamed by her weakness and hating this situation. Hot tears stung her eyes.

"Kay?"

The door opened, and she knew what he saw. A black-and-blue woman, naked, clinging to the side of a tub she couldn't even climb out of. Why couldn't she have just died out there in the snow? Then it would have been all over. No more pain, no more shame, no more embarrassment…

"Ah, lady," he breathed, and she realized with horror that his mouth was right beside her ear. "Hold on," he murmured. "I'll get you out of there."

To her infinite relief, she felt towels settle over her body, felt him tuck them around her from her shoulders to her knees.

"It's okay," he said. "Hold on just another second."

Her heavy wet hair was lifted from her shoulders, and she felt him wrap another towel around her head.

"Now," he said gently, "I'm going to lift you as carefully as I can. I can't guarantee we won't lose a towel, but I'll try. Okay?"

"Okay," she said, hating herself, fighting down those awful, hot, helpless tears. "I'm sorry."

"Don't be sorry. No need. Every single person on this earth needs help sometimes."

She kept her eyes tightly closed as his arms worked their way gently around her. As she had feared, the towels slipped a bit and his callused hand met the smooth skin of her hip. He stopped at once and struggled to pull the towel back over her.

"Don't worry about it," she whispered finally. "Nothing you haven't seen anyway." And maybe humiliation would kill her right now.

"Nicer than most I've seen by far."

She realized he was trying to joke, probably to make her more comfortable. She bit her lip as he began to lift her. Inevitably his arms and hands found some of her bruises, and she caught her breath more than once.

But by and large the towels stayed in place, even if his skin did keep brushing hers. At least he was wearing long sleeves.

She expected him to set her on her feet, at which point her stupid modesty would fall with the towels to the floor, but he surprised her. Moving carefully, he carried her back into the living room and laid her on the couch. An instant later, the quilt settled over her.

"I'll get the sweats," he said. "Then I'll leave you to dress."

"Thank you." Finally she opened her eyes and watched as he went back to the bathroom. He returned quickly with the clothing and placed it on the coffee table. When she dared to glance at his face, her heart sank.

The stone facade had returned, as impenetrable as when she had first seen him. Worse, he wouldn't even look at her. She must repulse him. Damn, that hurt as much as anything.

She didn't know what kind of approval she was seeking from this man, but it sure didn't help to feel that she was just an ugly burden he wanted to be rid of.

But was that fair? He'd been so kind. She couldn't blame him if he found all her bruises repugnant, and found her repellant for not having been able to stand up to Kevin. Not when she felt that way herself.

"Let me know when you're done." And then he disappeared into the back of the cabin.

Stifling further groans for fear he would come riding to her rescue again, she managed to sit up and work the towels over the parts of her that were still wet. Like a brand, the remembered warmth of his hand seemed to remain on her hip. The touch, she realized with a kind of wonder, hadn't repulsed her, or made her want to flee.

That alone marked a major change in her course. Since Kevin, she had hated to be touched in any way. *Any* way. Thoughtfully, she put her hand over the spot and pressed. That accidental touch had actually felt *good*.

Which left her with something to think about as she worked her way into the sweat suit and tried to roll up the legs so she wouldn't trip on them.

"Clint? I'm decent."

He returned at once to gather up the towels, except for the one wrapped haphazardly around her head. He paused, looking at her, and seemed almost hesitant.

"Do you," he finally asked, "need help with your hair?"

She wanted to tell him no, to just let it be, because that would have been her instinctive response before. But something had changed. Something had shifted, and she couldn't even tell what had happened.

"Would you mind?" she asked just as hesitantly.

"No." Short and brief. "Hold on a second."

He took the other towels away, and then a couple of seconds later he returned with a fresh towel and a comb.

"Sorry I don't have a brush," he said, indicating his short hair with a gesture. "I'll be careful."

He walked behind the sofa and spread the dry towel over her shoulders. Only then did he remove the damp one from her hair. She felt the heavy weight fall to her shoulders.

"Now lean back until you're comfortable."

She followed directions, feeling almost as if she was split in two, the old Kay watching in amazement as the new Kay let a man comb her hair.

He was almost unbelievably gentle. When he found a knot, he worked it carefully, never yanking.

"Where'd you learn to comb hair?" she asked finally.

"Horses," he said, with something like a short laugh. "Manes tangle. Your hair's a lot finer, though."

"It tangles really badly."

"Not that badly." He kept working, taking his time, taking it easy with her. She actually enjoyed his attention and could scarcely believe it.

"So," she asked after a few more minutes, "do you have horses?"

"I own a couple, but I have a friend take them over the winter. I like to ride a lot, but not in the winter, so he sees to it they get plenty of exercise."

"Sounds like a good friend."

"He is. It's also his business, so I don't have to feel bad about stabling them with him. He's really good with them. They come back every spring fat and happy and a pleasure to ride. I don't have his touch, so every summer I manage to work some kinks into them, and every winter he irons them out."

She laughed a little. "What kind of kinks?"

"Oh, they get a little stubborn. A bit fussy. Gideon's tried to figure out what I do wrong, but so far he just fixes things and can't tell me where I mess up."

"So he knows what to do right but can't tell you how to do it right, too? That's weird."

His hands stopped combing, just briefly, then resumed their work. "Well, actually, he does tell me something."

"What's that?"

"He keeps saying, 'Clint, you just gotta open your heart to those mares.' Damned if I know what he means."

Oh, Kay thought with a pang, that made *so* much sense. And it was a pity he didn't understand. Or maybe he didn't want to understand. She could sure grasp not wanting to give heart-space to someone or something.

"There you go," he said. "I have a rubber band if you want it off your shoulders until it dries."

"Thanks, it's fine. The fire should dry it fast." And she was so sorry he was done combing. The attention had touched her in ways little had in a long time.

"Feel better?" he asked.

"Tons. It's so nice to be clean again."

"Yup, that helps a lot."

No doubt he spoke from experience, especially since he sounded so certain, but she didn't feel she could ask.

After he'd cleaned up the mess from her bath, he brought her another mug of coffee. "Still no power," he remarked. "I'd lay odds at this point it'll be out all night."

"Well, I certainly feel cozy enough."

He gave her that half-smile again, the one that didn't quite crack the stone. He'd pulled back again from the place they'd nearly reached before her bath. She relaxed a little more, glad that the barriers were back in place. She didn't want the intimacy they'd shared because of her bath and hair any more than he did.

Or so she told herself. But she wasn't quite believing it anymore.

And that scared her as much as the lurking threat of Kevin.

Chapter 6

As soon as he could think of a good excuse and didn't think it was too soon, Clint announced he was going back out to check for wind damage.

Stepping out into the icy blow both shocked him and relieved him after the heat in the cabin. And not just the heat from the fire.

Crap. It was the mildest cuss word in his vocabulary, but he settled for it largely because he was making a strenuous effort to avoid using language that might singe Kay's ears. For a woman who'd been through all that she had, there seemed to be an innocence at her core. Maybe a kind of naiveté. Although he had to admit his own blighted soul hardly provided a good measuring stick by which to gauge anyone else.

The blowing snow that stung his skin, along with the wind that could suck the life out of him in a matter of minutes if he shucked his jacket, at least brought some balance back.

He was a monster. He was the bad guy. He was Kay's worst nightmare, even if he was pretending to be her savior. What Kevin had done to her was nothing compared to the things he himself was capable of. Things he'd done. Things he'd had to do.

Although *had* was a word choice he still wasn't comfortable with. Yeah, he'd done what was necessary to follow his orders and complete his missions. At the time, that had seemed to be enough. It was only later, during the dark night of the soul, that an honest man had to ask himself why he'd allowed himself to be twisted to such ends.

Why the hell he hadn't just drawn a line in the sand and said "No." Because at some point, you had to take responsibility for your actions.

Yeah, as he'd said to her, everyone did the best they could at the time, but that rang hollow in some deep interior place. For him, at any rate, which was why his book on Just War Theory set off so many negative reactions. Because he didn't just write about the responsibility of nations, he wrote about the responsibility of *individuals*. Like himself.

He cussed again, letting out a stream of colorful words in several languages, and kicked at the snow as if he could release some of his spleen on nature.

Okay, so he'd had to help the woman. No escaping that. But *desire* her? God almighty, she was wounded, damaged, frightened—and justifiably so. What the hell was wrong with him, that he could find her so attractive? And he didn't want to blame it on being alone too long, didn't want to blame normal male urges, none of that stuff, because in the end, *he* was responsible for everything he felt and said.

That was why he had a brain. To turn away from temptations that might condemn him to an even deeper circle of hell.

He bent and scooped up snow in both bare hands, squeezing it so hard some of it melted and water ran between his fingers. He held it until his hands turned numb, then dropped it.

Control. That was all it took, and he'd been working on his self-control for a long time. It ought to be strong enough to deal with this distraction.

Ought to be.

"Hah," he said, the word snatched away by the angry wind. Sharing his cabin with that woman was proving to be a circle of hell all its own, because the beast in him was waking, the beast with the primal urges.

Turning suddenly, he stalked around the cabin, making one last check, then re-entered. Kay sat up quickly, then relaxed when she saw him.

"Don't relax," he said shortly. Her eyes widened. Good.

He kicked off his boots and dumped his jacket. Then he went to sit in his chair, facing her tensely across the coffee table.

"What's wrong?" she asked.

"Me."

"Are you sick?"

"Sicker than you know." He closed his eyes, then decided to go ahead and do it, just do it. He needed her to look at him with the fear he deserved. It would help keep him in line.

"I'm going to tell you something," he said finally.

"I'm listening."

"You should be very afraid of me." He heard her gasp.

Then, her voice, hesitant, "Why?"

He opened his eyes, sure the bottomless abyss of his soul must show there. He sure hoped it did. "Because I'm a monster.

"What do you mean?"

"You have no idea what I'm capable of. I make Kevin look like a tyro. I'm a trained killing machine. I've maimed, I've terrorized and I've killed. The fact that it was my job is no excuse. I *know* what I'm capable of, and Kevin doesn't even begin to approach my capacity for evil."

Her blue eyes had grown huge, but he was annoyed to see that she didn't shrink back.

He leaned forward. "Do you think," he asked in a low voice, "that we get to check our consciences at the door and never accept responsibility for the things we do under color of war?"

"I...never thought about it."

"Most people don't. Why should they? They never have to walk into hell. But those of us who have...we're never the same again. That's why so many vets have all kinds of psychological problems, you know. Because society breaks the contract."

"What contract?"

"The one that says 'We sent you. Do this in our name, and we waive all the usual moral rules for you.' Which implies a responsibility shared among all of society, don't you think?"

She nodded, still wide-eyed.

"They promise us an absolution they can't give. Whether they give us parades or put flashy bumper stickers on their cars, tie yellow ribbons on things or call us heroes, they *cannot* give us absolution because it's not theirs to give." He ran his fingers impatiently through his short hair.

"So they say, 'Go do this in our names, and we'll call you heroes.' But what they really mean is, 'Go out and fight for us, do horrible things in our name, drop your civilized veneer and then come home and act like it never happened. Act like *we* aren't responsible for what we asked you to do. And sure as hell don't ever tell us about it.'"

"Oh, Clint…"

He brushed aside the soft sounds of sympathy. "But there's another part, too. Those of us who do the dirty work not only have to live with it, but we have to accept the responsibility for having done it. We don't get to squeeze out of it. We see it every time we close our eyes. And we have to ask ourselves why we just didn't say no."

"How could you have said no? I mean…you don't know what it's going to be like until it's too late."

"Well, that's the trick, you see. They found out during the Second World War that men are actually opposed to killing each other. Only one in four soldiers in battle actually fired their guns."

"Wow."

"Exactly. So they developed a gaming system. Haven't heard about that, have you? They train you on lifelike video games before you ever hit the field. You wouldn't believe how many soldiers I've heard say, 'It was just like a video game. Until afterward.' Afterward, when they start picking up the pieces of bodies. But by that time, you're in a kill-or-be-killed situation, which is all the push you need to cross the line. And then the next line. And the next. And then those lines will never exist again."

"No?"

"No. Because afterward you get pissed. And scared. And a whole bunch of other things that push you past the boundaries of basic morality. Your buddies are dead or maimed. You're being attacked. And you stop thinking, because you can't afford to think. Not until much later."

At least this time she didn't try to say anything.

"And some of us lucky ones get extra training, extra brainwashing, and get sent into situations where we do things the movies try to clean up and make look heroic. But believe me, there's no heroism in it. You get there one step at a time, and once you're in it, there's no way out. So you just do it. Mostly because if you don't, your buddies could pay for it. No soldier ever fought for a flag, or for mom and apple pie. No, we fight for the guy beside us."

She closed her eyes for a moment, then opened them. She ought to be avoiding his gaze, but she wasn't. Was she crazy?

"I'm so sorry," she whispered. "So, so sorry."

A kind of frustration filled him. "Don't you get it, Kay? I'm telling you I'm a monster."

"I don't think a monster would be telling me all this with such obvious self-loathing."

He swore, and this time he didn't spare her ears. Worse, she didn't even flinch.

No, instead she showed a spark of the fire that had been missing since he found her, a fire he'd been sure must have been there all along, because she had *survived*.

"You need to stop doing this to yourself," she said hotly. "The world is full of people who've been pushed into the same situation. That doesn't make any of you monsters."

"No? Then what the hell does it make us?"

"People," she said flatly. "Ordinary people. People shaped by extraordinary circumstances. Do you think I've never thought of slipping a knife between Kevin's ribs? Do you think I've never fantasized about killing him? Oh, I've planned it a dozen ways. What does that make *me*? Another monster?"

"*You* didn't do it."

"Mostly from lack of opportunity." She looked down and picked at a bit of fuzz on the sweatshirt she wore. "I plan to do it if he comes after me again. I want to get a gun."

Something inside him cracked a bit, a painful crack. "Don't do that," he said hoarsely.

"Why not? I can't keep living like this."

"You won't want to live with yourself afterward. Trust me on that. You will *hate* yourself. Let someone else take care of it."

"Who else? No one else has taken care of it except that time he went to jail, and then he just came back."

"I'll do it then, dammit!"

"No!" She almost screamed the word at him. "No. You have enough to deal with. Do you think I want Kevin on your conscience, too?"

That crack inside him became wider, deeper, and so painful he could have ripped the cabin apart with his bare hands. "Don't trust me," he said again, his chest so tight he could barely squeeze the words out. "Don't ever, ever trust me."

"I already trust you."

"Don't. You don't begin to understand the rage I live with. I've seen some of my buddies, some of the best people in the world, take it out on their wives and kids. *I am not to be trusted.* Under any circumstances. This demon inside me could burst out at any moment."

She bit her lower lip and looked down, pulling another bit of lint free, then looked up and met his eyes again. "I'll take my chances."

He swore and jumped up from his chair, unable to hold still another minute. He paced the room like a panther on the prowl. He hoped she could see the building danger in him, hoped that she would just shut up and let him walk it off.

Damn, he wanted to pound his fist into a wall, but he wasn't idiot enough to break his own hand just to break the cycle of his thoughts. Finally he came to a halt as far as he could get from her without leaving the room, faced the wall and pressed his forehead to the rough wood. He breathed deeply, leashing the monster again. Because he had to. Because he needed to. Because every time he leashed the damn thing, it got a tiny bit easier.

He hoped letting it out had scared her good. For her own protection. But now he had to put the monster back in its cage.

Then, freezing him in place, he felt a touch on his forearm.

"Clint," she said softly. "Clint…"

It was too late. Turning, he wrapped her in his arms and pulled her tightly to him, crushing her mouth beneath his.

Because, heaven help him, he needed the human touch. The human warmth. The feeling that he was still, somewhere deep inside, good enough for someone.

She astonished him. After her first gasp and a helpless groan that barely penetrated his awareness—that almost, but not quite, reminded him that she hurt all over—she raised her arms and wrapped them tightly around his neck.

As if she never wanted to let go.

Oh, God, the crack grew even wider, the pain flooding him, and in an instant he became helpless before the need, the anguish, the hunger.

That helplessness shocked him back to his senses. He couldn't afford to lose control. Never again.

Struggling against needs that bound him more tightly than even her arms, he tore his mouth from hers, then forced her arms from around his neck. He pulled back, just a few inches, but enough for salvation.

Her eyes opened slowly, sleepily. Her mouth looked bruised now, too, and he hated himself.

"Clint…"

"I need to cool down. I'm going outside."

Something sad flickered across her face, but she nodded. He made himself wait just long enough to be sure she was able to get back to the couch.

Then he strode out into the storm he never should have come in from to begin with.

Idiot!

* * *

Kay didn't know what to do. She'd thought she had lost the ability to feel pain for anyone else. She'd thought she had put her softer emotions in as tightly locked a vault as possible, leaving her to live on a steady diet of fear and caution.

But now she discovered that she was still capable of feeling as much pain for another person as for herself. Maybe even more.

And the person she felt it for was out there in the storm, probably trying to put his demon back in its cage.

She had her own demon, but suddenly she felt it was nowhere near as bad as what Clint was dealing with. The amount of self-hatred he'd shown her had been frightening. For all she beat herself up about what she had done or hadn't done with Kevin, how she had failed herself and shamed herself by not being stronger, nothing she had been through could possibly compare with what Clint was going through right this very minute.

And she didn't know what she could do to help. That pained her, too. Here he was, taking care of her, promising her protection, and she couldn't do a thing for him. If anything, she seemed to be awakening the very things he was trying to put to sleep.

At that moment, if there hadn't been a storm outside, she would have fled just to spare him. Except that would spare him nothing, nothing at all. He would hate himself if she ran, hate himself even more if she got lost—or, worse, *caught*—out there.

God, the helplessness Kevin had made her feel didn't even come close to this.

Finally she couldn't stand sitting there thinking any longer. Biting her lip against the aches and pains, she stood and went into the kitchen. Maybe she could cook something for dinner. Something to show her appreciation for the way he'd taken care of her.

Just one little thing to tell him that he mattered, too.

"What are you doing?"

His voice startled her, and she turned as quickly as she could. She hadn't heard him come in, but now he stood in the kitchen doorway, filling it, and from what she could see by the dimming light of the propane lantern she'd carried in here with her, he didn't look exactly happy.

"Cooking," she said, hoping she sounded steadier than she suddenly felt.

"You shouldn't be doing this. You're still a mess. You could get hurt."

"I'm fine. It's not that strenuous. I found a can of clams, so I'm just making chowder."

He stepped in closer. "Smells good." He sounded grudging.

"It'll smell even better in a couple of hours." She reached for the cutting board to dump the last of the diced potatoes into the pot, but he snatched it before she could lift it and scraped the potatoes in for her.

"Don't forget your ribs."

"Thanks." She wanted to ask if he was feeling any better but decided that would be foolhardy. He was so close now that she could have reached out to touch him—*would* have done so, if it were up to her, because she yearned to re-establish the link they had been building, however warily. But that was all shattered now, she supposed. And there was no telling, given what had happened earlier, how he would react to her touch. "I prefer," she started, then had to clear her throat. "I prefer to make it with half and half, but milk will do. I'll just add a bit of butter for richness."

"I'm sure it'll be wonderful."

She tried a smile and was relieved when there seemed to be a slight softening in his face. Maybe he'd walked off some of his mood, although it wouldn't help except to postpone things. But sometimes, as she had learned, even a break would do.

"What can I do to help?" he asked.

"Find me a pot lid. I couldn't look in the lower cabinets, I'm afraid. And this needs to simmer for a while."

"You'll need to step back a bit."

She did, and he bent to pull a lid out of the cabinet beside the stove. He put it on the pot. "Anything else?"

"That's it for now."

He turned the lantern, which sat on a small island, and pumped it so that it burned brightly again. Then he looked at her. "You need to get back to the sofa, Kay. You're looking pale."

"How can you even tell in this light?" she asked a bit querulously, but her body was telling her the same thing. How long would it take to get her strength back? she wondered. She definitely felt shaky and suspected rubbery knees awaited right around the corner.

Without a word, he took her elbow gently and guided her back to the couch. So where had the monster gone?

Had he buried it temporarily in the snow outside? Probably. She was good at burying things sometimes, too.

After he saw her settled, he disappeared into the kitchen, only to return about ten minutes later with fresh coffee for both of them.

"Thanks." She accepted hers with pleasure. She'd thought about making a pot, but in a strange kitchen, feeling as she did right now, she'd opted to stick with something for dinner. Finding the coffee and then wondering how he preferred to make it had seemed like one task too many.

"The chowder will need to be stirred from time to time," she told him. "Just letting you know, in case I fall asleep again."

"I can do that."

She had not the least doubt that this man could do just about anything he put his mind to. That alone was intimidating. He was obviously extremely smart, and experienced in so many things. What did she have to say for herself? Very little. She could wait tables, she could run, she could even cook decently. Beyond that, she had no accomplishments to show for twenty-six years on this planet.

A sigh escaped her.

"Is something wrong?" he asked at once.

Some monster, she thought. His concern for her was overwhelming, and certainly more than she had known since her grandmother died. She decided to be blunt. "I was just thinking about how little I've accomplished with my life."

"That probably depends on how you're measuring it."

A little laugh escaped her, and her ribs twinged. "*Now* you sound like a professor. Or maybe a shrink."

"Shrinks are good. Some of them, anyway. They don't let us make excuses, they just tell us that we aren't doing as badly as we think, and while we're at it, maybe we need to change some things."

"You've been to one?"

"Extensively."

"Doesn't seem like he helped you much."

"I'm still here."

She almost winced at that, because of what it said about the parts of hell he'd visited in order to reach this point in his life. Suicide? It had crossed her mind a couple of times. She suspected it had crossed his even more.

"Well, what would a shrink tell me, then?" she challenged him.

"I don't know you well enough to even guess. But I'm fairly certain she would tell you to stop beating yourself up over the things Kevin did."

"And if I managed that?"

"That it's time to look for new ways of dealing with this problem."

"What ways?" The words burst out of her. "Don't you think I've tried?"

"I'm sure you have."

"Then what?"

He raised his hand, absently covering his lower face as he thought. "Shall I tell you what I can offer?"

"Sure." She doubted it was much, short of killing Kevin, and she'd been serious when she'd said she didn't want him to be responsible for that.

He dropped his hand. "If we don't put that sucker away for life, then I know some people who can get you a new identity. Everything, top to bottom. Impenetrable. That jerk would never find you again."

She felt her jaw drop a little. "Really? That's possible?"

"It's more than possible. People do it all the time. But the folks I know are experts who can do it all legally, and so well your new persona would be seamless."

For some reason she found that amazing. Yes, she knew about fake identity cards. In fact, as a waitress, she'd learned to look out for them. She knew some people changed their identities to escape a crime, but they often got caught anyway. And she didn't believe a thing she saw in the movies about how to hide under an alias. "How is that possible?"

"You need to know the right people in the right places. And I'm not talking about the underworld here."

"Fantastic," she whispered. "But how could I pay for it? It must be expensive."

"It would be free. A favor. But first, let's see if we really need to go that far. If we can get Kevin into a six-by-eight cell for life, none of that will be necessary."

"Maybe not." She sighed again, turning the possibilities around in her mind. "I could really be someone else?"

"If that's what you need. So let's say you could be someone else, Kay. What would you do with a truly fresh start?"

It still boggled her mind. "I...I don't know. I never thought about it."

"Well, think about it now. Because one way or another, before you leave this house, you're going to have a new life."

She almost shivered when she saw the determination in his eyes. This man was capable of things she could barely imagine, and she believed all the way to her bones that he accomplished *any* task he set for himself.

"I'd save up money and go to college," she said.

"I'd fix it so you could get financial aid. Scholarships and loans. No reason to wait. You'd have to work while you're in school, like most students, but you wouldn't have to save up first."

"That would be amazing."

"So what would you do with that gift? It's not one many of us get."

"I know that. I'd want…I'd want to help people somehow."

One corner of his mouth lifted. "There's a beautiful soul locked up inside all that fear."

"I don't know about that. It's just that…" She hesitated. "The places I've been, I'd want to make it easier for other people who are there, too. Kids in foster care. Battered women. I know what desperation is like."

He nodded. "Life hasn't crippled you yet."

That comment interested her. She turned it around, thinking about it, and finally said, "Maybe not."

"Definitely not," he said firmly. "You've been hobbled, but not crippled. Once we take care of that bastard, the sky's the limit for you."

Did he really mean that? How could he? As he said, he didn't know her very well. But still, she liked what he seemed to see in her, something beyond a terrified woman forever on the run. Not just a rabbit in perpetual flight from a fox. She smiled a little, liking the way that made her feel. Almost like an infusion of emotional strength. "Thank you."

"Just calling it the way I see it."

Moving with care, she pulled her legs up beneath her and sat cross-legged. Once she achieved the position, it felt good, moving stress points around and giving a break to some of the more painful spots.

But the best thing of all was that for the first time in a long time, she actually felt the stirrings of hope.

And all because of the stone-faced, self-confessed "monster" who sat across from her. Maybe *he* wasn't as crippled as he thought, either.

Chapter 7

The storm wound down overnight, bringing a morning that sparkled with brilliant sunlight. The power still hadn't come back on, though, although it hadn't been terribly missed. They'd managed just fine without it. The fire had kept the living room warm, and the propane stove in the kitchen made it possible to cook and make hot beverages. What more did you need? Kay wondered.

She had pulled back the curtains to look out, noting that the wind had buried the driveway again, the one that deputy Micah had plowed out only yesterday. She wondered if Clint had some kind of plow, too. She couldn't imagine trying to clear all of that by hand.

"Get away from the window."

Kay jumped and turned swiftly, dropping the curtain. Clint had just returned from the back of the house, where he'd evidently gone to change into a fresh flannel shirt and jeans.

"What? Why?"

"Just stay away from it."

"What aren't you telling me? Has something happened?"

"Phones aren't working."

Even she could tell that was misdirection. "Clint? Don't lie to me. For God's sake, don't lie. Do I have a reason to be afraid of being seen?"

He hesitated long enough to give her an answer.

"Oh God," she said shakily. Feeling suddenly weak, she tried to stagger to the couch. He crossed the room in a flash to steady her. When she was sitting, he squatted in front of her.

"What do you know?" she asked on the merest breath. "What didn't you tell me? Clint, I *have* to know."

After a moment, he nodded. "When you gave me the description of Kevin's car yesterday, I thought I might have seen it."

"When? Where?"

"Right after I found you. I was carrying you to my truck. Now, before you panic, let me tell you I'm not *sure* it was him. I wasn't paying that close attention, because I was more concerned with you. Plus, the snow had started to blow pretty badly, so I didn't have a clear view. But a car *like* his passed us and slowed. At the time I thought it was someone going up the road to my neighbor's place."

"Oh God." Her stomach sank like a stone. Had Kevin really come that close to tracking her down? Had she been saved only by a matter of minutes and this man? "Oh God."

"Kay, I can't be sure it was him. Neither can you."

"But you're worried enough that you don't want me by the window."

"That's just common sense. In case. We don't know that he knows where you are."

"But he *could* know I'm here."

His reluctance was obvious when he nodded. "Don't worry, lady. I won't let him get to you."

"How are you going to prevent that?"

His faced hardened again. "I have ways."

She closed her eyes, feeling the panicked wings of terror beating throughout her body. Not Kevin. Not again. Not as she'd just begun to hope.

"Kay." Clint touched her arm. She opened her eyes reluctantly. "I told Micah about it. They'll be watching like hawks, too. But I'm going to take some more precautions."

"What kind?"

"I'm going to make sure he can't get into the house without waking the dead."

Still shaken, she watched as he kept his word. Below each window, he placed hazards that would trip anyone who tried to climb in. On the rear and side doors, she watched him set up what he called "trip wires." If anyone opened them from the outside, a noisy shower of objects would fall.

He gave the front windows, the ones where she would be most exposed, extra treatment; he nailed them shut. With each blow of the hammer, she winced, realizing that safety had been an illusion, that once again she was in a prison of terror.

"Why didn't you tell me?" she asked. "Why?"

"Because you weren't in danger of any kind during the storm. You needed to rest."

"I needed a lie?"

"It wasn't a lie. I can't be sure it was him. Nor can you. I'm just taking precautions."

"I want a gun."

"I keep them locked up. For good reason. And I don't need one to take care of this guy."

"But what if *I* do?"

He shook his head. "Too dangerous."

"Dammit, Clint!"

He just shook his head again. Then he squatted in front of her and took her shoulders. "Listen to me. Guns are dangerous. What happens if you get scared in the dark and think I'm him?"

"I'd never mistake you for him."

"When you're scared, everything looks like a threat. Do you have any training?"

"No."

"Can you be absolutely sure you'd shoot? Because if you don't, and he gets close enough, then you've armed *him*. Trust me on this one, Kate, if he's fool enough to try to get in here, he'll have his hands fuller than he can possibly imagine, and I don't need a gun to make him regret it."

"Maybe *you* don't."

"Okay, you want a weapon? How about a fireplace poker? Or a tire iron? You can hide it right here beside you, and if he ever gets that close, you can do enough damage with one blow to put him down until I can take him out."

She finally accepted his reasoning, though it didn't make her happy. "Something he can't pull out of my hand. He's strong."

"I'll figure it out."

"But he could still hit me first."

He shook his head, his gray eyes never wavering from hers. "Kay, I'd have to be dead to let him get that close."

God, what a thought. What an image he painted of himself. She couldn't help it. Terror was driving her, and he was the only anchor she had. She leaned forward and wrapped her arms around him, clinging.

At first he froze, as if he'd become the stone he pretended to be. Then, almost cautiously, he slipped his arms around her, gently, oh so gently, and just let her cling.

"I'll protect you," he whispered. "I swear it."

But at what cost? It was a question she didn't dare ask.

By midmorning it was easy to see that Clint had become restless. She wished she could feel that much energy, but evidently her body still demanded rest. Finally he went to one of the windows and looked out.

"I need to plow the drive."

"Do you need to go somewhere?"

"If it becomes necessary, yes." He turned from the window and looked at her. "You'll be safe," he said. "Nobody can approach this house right now because of the snow. Somehow I think it would take more guts than Kevin has to hike his way in here."

"Really?"

"A man who beats up on women is a coward."

"Or crazy," she said quietly.

"Do you think he's that crazy?"

"I don't know."

"Then ride in the truck with me. It won't take long. Just let me get the thing started so the cab is warm for you."

"Thank you." She let a sigh of relief escape her. Yes, it might be beyond Kevin to hike his way through all this snow, but a few years ago she would have thought it beyond him to pursue her across the country, too. Not only had he done that three times now, but he'd actually abducted her. Crazy? Yeah, he was crazy.

He went outside and started the truck. She could hear it roar a bit at first, then listened as it came around to the front of the house. The vehicle sounded none-too-happy about the volume of snow it had to push.

Then Clint stomped back in, shaking snow off his boots. "Let me find you something to put on your feet. And I have an extra jacket, though it'll probably swallow you whole."

"That'll just make it warm," she said with a smile. For some reason she felt like smiling. Maybe because he cared enough about her feelings not to leave her alone. Maybe because she was actually going to get out into the sun and fresh air for a little while.

He brought her several pairs of thick socks and knelt to pull them on her. "My feet are way too big," he said. "If I gave you a pair of my boots, you'd trip for sure. So I'll carry you to the truck, okay?"

She didn't mind the idea at all, oddly enough. She looked at the top of his dark head as he worked the socks onto her and felt a swelling appreciation for him. He could be incredibly kind and thoughtful, and he cared for her as if she were as precious as Limoges china, and as delicate. Nobody, absolutely *nobody,* had ever done that for her. Not even her earliest memories of her mother included this kind of care.

After the socks came a gray nylon parka. He zipped it up, even though it bagged on her and fell almost to her knees. Then he rolled up the sleeves, no easy task, but at least her hands were free.

Next he offered her big, thick blue mittens. She managed those by herself and then giggled at the way they flopped loosely at the ends of her fingers.

Even Clint smiled. "I'm sure you must be in there somewhere."

"That's the story, anyway."

At that, a chuckle escaped him. Then, without further ado, he swept her up, one arm beneath her knees, the other around her shoulders. It never ceased to amaze her that he was so strong. And where that had once frightened her, now it made her feel safe.

Probably a dangerous way to feel, she thought. She couldn't trust *herself* right now, couldn't trust her own feelings, and he clearly wanted no part of human entanglements. The only thing this man could offer her was more pain, just a different kind of pain.

He carried her out to the truck and deposited her in the already-warming cab. He went back to lock the front door, then climbed in beside her.

His vehicle was an older Suburban, heavy and powerful, but it still resisted a bit when it bit into the deep, heavy snow. He kept it in low gear and managed the manual transmission like a pro as he steadily moved forward and back, clearing away the snow with the plow blade attached to the front.

"She gets cranky about this," he remarked. "But then, she's not a snow plow."

"How long is your drive?"

"About eight-tenths of a mile. You'll know when we get to the end because there'll be a wall left by the plow that went through during the night."

"The plow already came?" Her heart lurched a bit as she realized the roads were now open. Kevin, if he knew where she was, could come at any time.

"I heard it about four this morning. It'll probably be back later, too, and I'll have to bust out again."

"Do you have to do this often?"

"Depends. We've been getting more snow than usual the last couple of years. There've been winters, though, when I haven't had to do this but two or three times."

It took nearly a half hour, but they finally cleared the right side of the driveway and reached the wall he'd promised. Clint put the car in Park and muttered.

"What's wrong?" she asked.

"I just need to loosen that mess a bit. Stay put."

So she waited while he climbed out, opened the back of the truck and pulled out a heavy-duty shovel. She hated sitting there, doing nothing as he started chopping at the huge snowbank the plow had pushed across the end of his driveway. It looked hard. It was nearly as high as he was tall, and she could only imagine the effort he was expending trying to loosen it.

But finally he seemed satisfied the truck could do the job. When he climbed back into the cab with her, he was sweating from the heavy labor.

"Here we go," he said. He backed up about twenty feet, then floored the accelerator. "Hang on."

She braced in time. The Suburban hit the wall of snow hard, jerking her a bit against her seat belt, but she managed to stifle a cry as her bruises shrieked. A moment later they burst through, and he pushed the snow all the way to the far side of the road, slamming it into the snowbank over there.

He looked at her as he backed up again into his own driveway. "Once more," he said. "Can you handle it?"

She nodded, this time bracing even harder. "This could be fun, under other circumstances."

A laugh escaped him. "Yeah, if you weren't already so sore."

Once again he broke through what was left of the snow pile and drove the snow across the road. Then he performed a three-point turn and headed back up the driveway, this time clearing the other side.

"Are you okay?" he asked, when they finally pulled up in front of the house.

"Yeah. I'm fine." Except that tensing again and again had once again made her aware of every bruised muscle in her body. The pain would pass, though, and she didn't want to tell him.

But Clint was a perceptive man. Little escaped him. When he came around to lift her out and take her inside, he scanned her face. "What hurts?"

"Just some of the bruises."

"Not your ribs?"

"I can't even feel those anymore."

A little smile danced in his eyes. "Next time stay in the house."

"I don't think so."

The smile in his eyes reached his mouth. "Up to you." Then he scooped her up and carried her back inside. "I'll help you get unwrapped as soon as I stow the truck."

As soon as he closed the door behind him, she let a groan escape. Damn! She hadn't realized just how much of her hurt. Now all her muscles were shrieking again.

Biting her lip, she pulled the mittens off. Hot. She was getting hot in front of the fire. At least she could manage the jacket.

But it was so big that the task proved difficult. The zipper kept wanting to stick, because she couldn't grab the material to straighten it out. Finally she sagged backward and told herself to just wait.

But God, she was sick of being helpless. Helpless with Kevin, and now helpless in her own battered body. Every time she started to get a handle on her life again, Kevin appeared to blow it all up once again. And this time...this time he'd left her truly helpless. Unable to run, unable to even get out of a damn jacket.

Her anger was coming back, she realized. Replacing fear as her primary motivator, it began to seethe hotly inside her. Good. When she was angry, she took care of things. All kinds of things. Anger more than fear had enabled her to uproot herself again and again. Anger kept her going when fear would have frozen her.

Furious, she grabbed at the zipper again, and this time it slid downward more than half way. Now if she could just pull her arms out of these sleeves, she could get the damn thing off.

"Let me help you."

She hadn't heard Clint come back in and gasped at the unexpected sound of his voice. Then she said, "I want to do it."

"I can see that. And I don't blame you. But let's just do it the easy way this time."

Before she could protest, he pulled the stupid jacket right over her head.

"There. It's gone."

Relief and annoyance warred inside her. "Thanks. But I want to do things myself."

"I get it," he said. "Believe me, I get it. But when help is handy, what's the point of making yourself even sorer?"

Logic.

She didn't want logic right now. "Do you have any idea what this feels like?" she demanded. "I can't even get out of the tub on my own. Or pull off a stupid jacket."

"I know exactly what it feels like."

She paused in the middle of her angry tirade and looked at him. Something in his face made her heart sink. "How do you know?" she asked quietly.

He looked away, shrugging. "I've been wounded, too."

Oh God! She suddenly felt so small. Of course. Why hadn't she guessed that? Because she was so self-absorbed she couldn't feel a thing for anyone else?

"Do you want those extra socks off?" he asked after an uncomfortable moment.

"Please."

And this time she didn't object to his help or insist that she could do it herself. It seemed like a small bit of autonomy to give up for a man who had already done so much for her. A man who clearly needed to feel useful just as she did. A man whose reasons were much the same as hers, even if probably far worse in degree.

"Thank you," she said when he'd removed all but one pair of socks.

"No problem. Maybe we'll get the power back soon."

A safe subject. "I'm not really missing it," she offered. "You have a cozy place here."

"I like it." He rose, socks in hand, and started to walk away. Then he looked back. "Take it easy on yourself, Kay."

"You're one to talk."

"Obviously." One side of his mouth lifted a bit. "Always easier to talk than do."

"Isn't that the truth." But she tried to smile back at him.

For a few seconds he didn't move. It almost seemed as if they were locked in each other's gazes, as if some quiet kind of understanding passed between them. Then he looked away as if he didn't want the connection to continue. "Oh, before I forget…"

He walked over to the door where he'd dumped his own outerwear. He bent to pick up something, and as he returned, she saw it was a large tire iron.

"I promised you a weapon. Hold it by the bent end so you can get a good grip."

She took it from him cautiously. With that simple gesture, he'd brought the nightmare back into the room. Slowly she looked up at him. "I need this to end."

He nodded. "I understand *that*, too."

She had absolutely no doubt that he did.

Clint couldn't settle, and he knew exactly why. Senses and instincts honed by so many years in dangerous situations wouldn't allow him to sit back and relax. Was it likely Kevin would try to come up to the house by way of the drive? Absolutely not. He had to know he would have no chance if he announced his arrival.

So that left hiking through the snow. It would be nice to think he wouldn't attempt it, but despite what he had said to Kay, Clint was convinced that Kevin was insane enough to try just that.

Why? Because to Clint, Kevin read like a man who had tired of the chase. Maybe it had excited him for a while to know he could find Kay when he wanted and show up to terrify the hell out of her. But he had moved well past that when he'd abducted her, had moved into a crazy place that said he was through with the chase and wanted to finish it for good, regardless of the consequences to himself.

Clint had studied abnormal psychology in some depth because it fascinated him. And he knew about obsessions, including sick obsessions.

The obsession dictated the actions, Clint thought. And Kevin's obsession could only be ended in one way.

What was more, once the obsession reached full blossom, as it apparently had with Kevin's abduction of Kay, then it goaded, pressed and drove, demanding resolution, and the faster the better. It could not be repressed for long.

Kevin would most likely come by night, under cover of darkness. In the wee hours, when he would assume everyone in the house was asleep. Well, Clint didn't plan to sleep. With that snow out there, Kevin's approach should be clear enough, unless he camouflaged himself. Which was always a possibility. Crazy did *not* equate to stupid. In fact, it was often the contrary, especially if crazy included an element of paranoia.

Even if Kevin hadn't grown paranoid as a result of being sent to prison, he was probably paranoid by now. With good reason, since he had to be aware that it was possible his victim had told the police she had been abducted, and that there might be dozens of people looking for him right now.

A sane man would disappear, but Kevin wasn't sane. Oh, he might be sane enough by legal standards, but he wasn't sane by any other standard. He was probably hiding somewhere, fighting his compulsion to end this, waiting just long enough to convince himself that people would believe he'd moved on.

But Clint wasn't going to fall for that one. So how long would the guy judge that he needed? Impossible to know for sure. Maybe a few more days. At most. Because his obsession would goad him past patience, too. He would want this over and done with.

And of course he would have no idea what a formidable opponent he would be facing once he entered the house.

Clint performed a mental checklist. The guy would wait, hoping the heat would lessen. Then he would want to observe the house for a while to figure out how many people were inside. He could do that while he waited, now that the storm was over.

But there was another wrinkle, too. Assuming that *had* been Kevin who'd driven by them on the road, how could Kevin be sure Kay was still in the house? Clearly, merely by turning around a few miles up the road and backtracking he would have figured out that Clint had taken her there to start with.

But how could he be sure she hadn't been taken elsewhere since then?

For one thing, it would be easy for *anyone* to find out if she was in the hospital. Equally obvious was the likelihood that Clint hadn't taken her anywhere else because of the storm. In fact, it was unlikely that Kevin, even if he'd been nearby, would have seen Micah come to the house, given the state of the roads.

So that left what? The fact that Clint had brought Kay to his place and still had her. The fact that the guy couldn't be sure the cops hadn't been advised of Kay's abduction and his own description. In fact, it was likely they had been. But the truth was, all of Kay's attempts to keep her presence secret had probably been wasted from the moment Kevin saw Clint rescuing her.

Clint almost swore, then remembered Kay was nearby. He didn't want to worry her, much less unleash a stream of questions he couldn't adequately answer.

So okay, another few days maybe, enough for Kevin to feel things had calmed down and plan a stealthy approach to the house. But that would be the max, because Kevin's internal demons would be driving him.

A couple of days.

Not very long.

Chapter 8

The phone rang in the early afternoon, announcing that at least part of the world had started to return to normal. Clint answered it and found Deputy Sarah Ironheart on the other end.

"Hey, Clint," she said cheerfully. Her husband, Gideon, kept Clint's horses for the winter, and despite himself, he'd become a part of the Ironheart family.

"Hi, Sarah."

"Micah said I needed to come by and take some photos of your guest."

Clint froze. His mind spun through a series of possibilities very fast. Then, "Sarah, I think it would be a very good idea right now if we didn't advertise that the law knows Kay is here."

She fell silent for a few seconds. "You think he's watching?"

"I think he'd be a fool not to be. And I want him to think the heat's off."

"Are you sure about that?"

"I promised her we'd end this. If you don't run across him on the roads, then the end is going to happen here. And frankly, the sooner the better. This guy strikes me as a mental case. He's not going to wait long."

Sarah didn't hesitate. "I could come in civvies and take her out of there."

"And what if he sees?"

"Good point. Okay. I'll talk to Micah and Gage, and see if we can't set up some loose surveillance. Or at least keep some cars near your place."

"My bet is that he won't come by road. And I don't want him scared off, because he'll just come after her another time."

"You believe that?"

"Absolutely. This guy is obsessed, and there's only one way to end it. And I honestly don't think at this stage in his obsession that he's willing to wait for her to move on again. Or even wait very long to come after her here. What if she disappears for real? I don't think he's willing to risk that."

"All right, then. We'll see what we can do to help without being seen. But don't be surprised if you get a call from Gage. He won't be happy."

"Gage has done enough undercover work in his life. He'll get it."

When he hung up, he found a very pale Kay watching him.

"I'm sorry I'm causing you so much trouble."

What had brought that on? He ran his conversation with Sarah back in his mind and remembered the phrase, *Frankly, the sooner the better.* He could well imagine how she'd taken that.

Ordinarily he would have let it pass without explanation. He cared very little about what most people thought of him, but somehow he already cared what Kay thought. Part of him reared up to object, but it didn't stand a chance, not against that look on her face. Especially when abuse had made her so vulnerable and left her feeling like something to be kicked to the curb.

"I just want you out of danger as soon as possible. That's not the same as wanting to get rid of you as soon as possible."

She nodded, but her expression didn't change. He guessed she didn't believe him. And then she asked, "So we're bait in a trap?"

"Maybe."

"There's no maybe about it. It's the best way to get at him."

Then she closed her eyes, as if that admission had taken the last of her strength, and all the vivacity that had begun to return to her seemed to drain away.

Hell. He didn't want to be responsible for this. He didn't want to make her feel bad, but he wanted even less than that for her to care enough that he *could* make her feel bad. There was no future in it for either of them. Best if she just perceived him as a weapon to use to get free of Kevin.

But the truth was, she was too nice to look at other people that way—even him. He'd seen it already, in her concern that *he* not wind up with Kevin on his conscience. As if his conscience would note the weight added to the tonnage it already carried.

He swore under his breath. The cracks inside were getting wider, and dammit, he wasn't sure he wanted to fill them up with cement again. He should have turned and walked out of the room. Immediately.

Instead, looking at her wan, sad face, something else took over, something visceral, and he walked toward her, not away from her. He'd never felt like this before about anything that didn't involve life and death, but somehow that woman's hurt seemed every bit as important to him as his own survival.

He sat on the couch beside her, then gathered her onto his lap as carefully as he could manage when every cell in his body wanted to play the caveman.

Her eyes flew open, and her lips parted in astonishment.

Quit now, he told himself. Stop!

But he couldn't. He simply couldn't. This woman made him helpless in ways he hated, in ways he couldn't fight. In ways that knocked his barriers flat.

He lowered his head, needing to kiss her. Needing to let her know that at least one person in this world didn't think of her as trash to be kicked and then kicked aside.

And this time he needed something far gentler than the earlier crushing kiss he'd given her. He needed to feel like he wasn't a monster.

As his mouth settled over hers, he felt her gasp, taking breath from him, saw her eyes widen, then flutter closed. She accepted his kiss as if she'd been waiting for it forever.

Ah, God, he thought as a new pain washed over him—a longing for an ordinary life, one that hadn't been blighted by his own failures. One that hadn't proved he was a monster at heart.

The yearning was so intense he couldn't break its grip. Just a few moments, he promised himself. Just this little bit and no more.

His lips moved gently on hers, asking, not demanding, a desperate question asked with utmost care, more care than he'd felt in a long time.

She answered tentatively at first, then as if she felt a hunger of her own. And she probably did. She must be as desperate as he was to know she wasn't just human garbage.

But it wasn't long before that caring yielded to something more basic. He didn't know who did it first, but their tongues met, engaging in an ancient dance. And with that shift, the hunger in him changed, too. His loins throbbed with long-denied needs, and the warning voice in his head yelled at him to stop.

But he couldn't stop. He needed this. He needed *her,* because somehow, in some way, she offered an absolution he couldn't find elsewhere.

She tore her mouth away, gasping for breath, but offered not a bit of resistance when he swooped in again for another kiss. He felt her melt against him, and almost before he knew what he was doing, his hand found her breast. Oh, man, she felt perfect against his palm, and he wanted to rip away the fabric that prevented him from feeling her skin. He found the strength, from somewhere, to keep his touch gentle when everything inside him screamed for him to just mount her now, to bury himself in the beauty and forgetfulness her body offered.

A small moan escaped her, and he felt her arch up against his hand, seeking more. Even through the thick fabric of the sweatshirt he could feel her nipple harden, just as he was hardening, and a flash of pure triumph ripped through him.

She wanted him, too. Every bit as much.

And all rational thought was fast flying out of his head, leaving him a prisoner of need.

His hand slipped up under the shirt, pushing it out of the way. More. He needed more, and he needed it *now*.

But just as he tore his mouth from hers and moved to take her exposed nipple into his mouth, she gasped and cried out.

Reality came back in one crashing instant. What the hell was he doing?

He lifted his head and looked into her frightened face. "Kay?" He struggled to regain his footing. "Did I hurt you."

"I'm sorry," she said, and huge tears began to fall. "I want...oh, God, I'm sorry." She struggled to pull the shirt down.

He helped, and when she wiggled as if to escape, he quickly helped her by shifting her to the far end of the couch. "Kay?"

"I'm sorry," she said, her voice breaking. "I'm sorry!" Then she turned her face against the back of the couch, and wracking sobs shook her.

What had he done? He didn't know. But the only thing he could think of to do for her now was to move away, to go sit in his own chair and give her space.

She cried for a while, and he just sat helplessly watching, figuring that even a hug might be taken amiss right now. He couldn't offer any solace at all, and that made him crazy.

"I'm sorry," he said, when her sobs began to ease. "I'm always doing that."

"Doing what?" she asked brokenly, her voice muffled against the back of the couch.

"Hurting you. I always hurt people." And he was damned if he knew how to fix it when he did.

"It wasn't you."

"What?" He was sure he'd misunderstood her.

She turned then, groaning a bit as she twisted until she faced him. "It wasn't you," she said in a tear-thickened voice. "Clint, don't blame yourself. It was me. *Me!*"

"You? You didn't do anything. *I* did."

"No, you don't get it. I wanted you to kiss me. But I can't. I *can't.*"

He was beginning to get it, and blackness seeped into the edges of his mind. "Why?"

"Because…" She gasped, almost a sob, and closed her eyes. "He raped me."

That did it. Clint rose, shoved his feet into his boots and then stepped outside into the bitter cold without even a jacket. He needed that cold, because right now his hands itched, absolutely *itched,* to wrap themselves around Kevin's throat. Or smash something. As if they had a mind of their own.

He couldn't let Kay see this. He couldn't risk expressing his rage to her. He didn't want to see her shrink from him again. He didn't think he could bear it.

But the urge to kill had never been stronger, and he had to walk it off. Rage clouded the mind, deadened the senses, and he couldn't afford that for Kay's sake, if nothing else.

He walked all the way around the cabin four or five times, not counting, fighting down the man he no longer wanted to be. The man he might have to become again to save Kay.

He looked up at the heavens, sending a blast of rage upward. What had that chaplain said to him? Oh, yeah, God has broad shoulders, and a curse can be a prayer, too. Yeah. Sure.

Except a lot of the time he didn't think God was listening. Nor should he, when you came right down to it. No reason to listen to Clint Ardmore, human monster. Probably already damned for eternity.

But what about Kay? he asked silently. What about Kay? She didn't deserve this.

A gust of wind blew snow into his face. No answer at all. But it reminded him that he was getting perilously close to hypothermia, and nice as it might be to just lie down in the snow and kiss off all the pain, he couldn't do that.

Not now. That woman inside was depending on him.

He took a couple of deep breaths, realizing that the rage was subsiding. He forced himself to let go of the last of his tension, as well.

Certain now of his self-control, he headed back inside. He kicked off his boots, his eyes seeking Kay. She was sitting stiffly on the couch and didn't even look around.

Oh, this was not good.

"Kay?"

"What?"

"Are you okay?"

"Whatever would make you think that?" she asked, her voice brittle.

Ah, hell. "What did I do now?"

"How could you have done anything? You were outside."

He wasn't buying it. In stocking feet he padded over and sat on the coffee table facing her. Some instinct told him that he needed to be close to her right now.

"Talk," he said.

"What's there to talk about?"

"Look, I'd tell you I'm sorry I kissed you, but I'd be lying. What I'm sorry about is what happened to you. And I feel so damn helpless. I can't fix it, Kay."

"Why would you think I expect you to fix anything?"

She wasn't looking at him, and little flags were beginning to pop up in his head. He knew a lot of psychology, and he began to suspect something.

"Do you think," he said slowly, "that I walked out of here because I was disgusted with you?"

"Of course you did! Don't bother trying to lie to me. I know what I am. Damaged goods. I can't even…I can't even…" Her voice broke, and she looked away. "I am so disgusting."

"Disgusting? That's the last thing you are. Do you want to know why I walked out of here? The real reason?"

She darted a look at him, then averted her gaze again.

"The real reason I walked out of here was that the monster inside me was getting loose. I wanted to kill someone. I wanted to kill Kevin. I did not, absolutely *did not*, walk out because I was disgusted with you. There is not one disgusting thing about you."

"Yes, there is," she said, her voice small.

"Why? Because you were raped? Like that was a choice you made? That dirt is all on Kevin, not on you. Even if life had forced you to stand on a street corner and turn twenty-dollar tricks, you wouldn't be disgusting. And there's most definitely *not* anything disgusting about you because you were raped."

She was silent so long that he began to fear he'd hurt her again. But then, still in a small voice, she said, "I think I'm worth more than twenty."

He almost chuckled in his relief, but caught himself, knowing it could well be exactly the wrong response. "More like a grand, maybe."

She looked at him from the corner of her eye. "There was a time I would have priced myself considerably higher."

"Well, I would, too, but I figured you'd think I was exaggerating."

Slowly she turned her head to look at him. A slight smile flitted over her mouth, but then the haunted expression returned. "I'm not worth anything right now."

"Why in the world would you think that?" But he suspected.

"Because I…can't. I wanted you to kiss me, and then I froze. I panicked. I'm…broken."

He sought words carefully. "Life breaks us all in one way or another. But if we try, we can put the pieces back together. It takes time. And we won't be exactly the same person we used to be. But we *are* whole again."

"Is that what you've done? Put yourself back together?"

"In my own rather crude way, yes. Still not done with the reconstruction, but working on it."

"With plenty of defensive walls."

He nodded, admitting it.

"I don't seem to be able to build those very well."

"I don't advise it, actually. Right now it doesn't seem to be working too well for me."

"What do you mean?"

But that was one question he wasn't prepared to answer, either to her or to himself. Because he didn't know what to make of all the fault lines that had begun cracking open inside him since this woman had come into his life. He didn't know if they would remain, or what his interior landscape might look like once the earthquake was over. Best to just remain silent.

She waited, then let it go. Unlike a lot of women he'd known, she didn't seem to feel a need to peck him open like a juicy seed until she knew every little nook and cranny inside him. He appreciated that, especially since he had some ugly nooks.

"I'm sorry," she said after a while. "I've barged into your hermitage, busted your solitude and created one emotional upheaval after another."

"Call it fresh air."

Her eyes widened. "What do you mean?"

He gave her a wry, pained smile. "Sometimes even hermits need to deal with something besides the cobwebs inside their own heads."

"Oh."

He could see that turning around in her head; then a cute, almost impish, smile appeared. "So I'm a feather duster?"

"Big-time, lady," he said. And finally he let a laugh emerge. "One really big feather duster."

He had to give it to her, she bounced back fast. He could see her muscles uncoiling, even as life began to return to her face.

That didn't mean the problems were over. By no means. Snakes had a way of going into hiding, then popping up again at unexpected moments. But Kay apparently had a resilient nature, and he liked that.

There might be some lessons there for him to learn, too.

Because, he finally admitted to himself, he was getting just a bit weary of nursing his own psyche.

The day remained sunny, the wind steadily growing calmer. Perfect conditions for Kevin, Clint thought as he walked from window to window. As the sun heated the snow on the roof, a few icicles began to grow around the eaves. Good. The more of them the better. If they grew big enough, they would become deadly. Handy weapons, and a bar to invasion.

He heard a clatter from the kitchen, and went there to find Kay struggling to pull out pots.

"Let me help with that," he said instantly. "What do you want to do?"

"Cook. I'm going to go crazy sitting on that couch worrying and thinking. I need to be busy, and you said you liked my chowder."

He should have thought of that. "The chowder was great."

"I think I saw a chicken in your refrigerator."

"Yeah, sometimes I actually cook myself."

She gave him a small smile. "Do you mind if I do?"

"Not a bit. I'll help, if you want." He pulled the chicken out and put it on a plate on the counter. "Kinda hard to wash it, though," he remarked. "No power, no running water, remember?"

"Oh, I forgot about that." She stared at the chicken, frowning faintly.

"Well, if we don't get power back soon, it'll spoil. I don't know how well the stuff in the fridge is keeping cool. So let's risk it. We just need to rinse it as best we can and then make sure it's fully cooked." He paused. "In fact, I probably ought to take what I can and put it in a snow bank to preserve it."

She touched the chicken. "It still feels pretty cold."

"But sooner or later, opening the fridge is going to warm it up too much." He sighed. "For a self-sufficient type, I'm standing here wondering why I never bought that generator I've been looking at for the last two years."

"We all have questions like that to ask ourselves."

"I suppose." He helped her wash the chicken by pouring water over it from the huge pot of water that still sat on the stove.

"Any lemons?" she asked him.

"As a matter of fact…" He opened his pantry, asking, "How many?"

"At least two."

She thanked him as she accepted them and placed them on the counter. "Pepper?"

He opened another cupboard and handed her the peppermill. "Salt?"

She nodded and took that, too. "Roasting pan?"

He dug that out of the back of another cupboard.

She regarded him. "Do you put *everything* away?"

"Why?" The question surprised him.

"Because I usually leave salt and pepper on my counter in easy reach."

"Oh." He shrugged. "Training. Stow everything."

"Navy?"

"Marines."

"Ah."

"But if you want, I can start leaving things out."

She gave him a humorous little smile. "And drive yourself crazy? I don't think so. I'll adapt." Her smile faded, and she bit her lip. "I guess I won't be here that long, anyway."

He didn't know how to answer that. If he agreed, she might think he was in a hurry to get rid of her again. And even if part of him thought that would be best for both of them, he didn't want to make her feel that way. If he disagreed, he might make her think she would never be able to get on with her own life. Lose-lose, he thought.

She turned back to the chicken, rubbing it with olive oil she'd found herself, sprinkling it inside with salt and pepper, then squeezing the lemons over the skin. To his surprise, she shoved the two halved and squeezed lemons into the cavity instead of tossing them.

"What's this?" he asked. "I've never seen anyone do that before."

"Lemon chicken," she offered. "I hope you like it."

"Sounds good." He didn't mind acting as if he were inexperienced in the kitchen if it made her feel good about what she was doing.

A sprinkle of salt on the outside of the chicken and then she placed it in the roasting pan. "All ready," she announced. "Thirty minutes at four-twenty-five, then fifty-five minutes at three-seventy-five."

He turned on the oven for her, letting it preheat. "Anything else?"

"Depends on what you want with it. I usually make this with yellow rice."

"Hey, I have that." He went back to the pantry and brought out a bag. "Too bad we can't use my rice cooker."

"You have a rice cooker?"

"I eat a lot of rice. Leftover habit from my time abroad."

She looked at him again, her eyes full of questions. He gave her credit for not asking them. "It'll cook well enough on the stove top," she said finally. "I don't have a rice cooker at…my place."

He noted she resisted the easy and obvious choice of the word *home*. That opened one of the cracks a little wider. This woman, he thought, didn't really have a home. Probably hadn't felt she had one for years. Maybe for a brief time with Kevin she had thought she was making one, but along with all the other things he'd done to her, the bastard had probably succeeded in making *home* a dirty word.

He stopped himself cold. He couldn't afford these thoughts. He sought his way back to safer ground. "I couldn't exist without one. It lets me make perfect rice without paying attention, and I tend to get distracted when I'm working."

She nodded but didn't say anything. Well, what was there to say?

"Anything else you need?"

"Not just yet. Vegetables later, if you have any."

"I've got a load of them in the freezer out in the garage. Probably most anything you could want."

"Then when it's time, we'll decide." Then she asked, "Am I keeping you from working?"

The answer was simple, though far from complete. "No power, no computer. So I get a holiday." But he also knew he couldn't keep on standing here and talking to her. Talking was dangerous. It created bonds. It might even reveal too many things he didn't want to reveal. But she'd expressed boredom, and he felt obligated to keep her occupied in some way. Occupied enough that she wouldn't notice his prowling as the evening grew closer.

"Listen," he said, "you like to read, right?"

"I love it."

"Then I've got something to show you."

Violating all his personal rules of privacy, he led her down the hallway and opened the door to his office. Ceiling-to-floor bookcases lined the walls, like battlements around his desk and computer. "If you see something you want and can't reach it, call me. I'll get it down for you."

"Thank you!" She looked genuinely pleased and excited. "I love books. I always wished I could have a library."

"Well, it's not exactly that big." But still way more than she could have when she was always being forced to move. He waved to the left. "Fiction on that side, nonfiction on the other. Most of it's in alphabetical order by author name, if you want to look for something in particular. Otherwise, happy browsing."

He left her then, needing to escape. Needing to get away from whatever it was in this woman that kept calling to him. Needing to get away from watching her explore the inner sanctum where he had never allowed anyone before.

Some might think that odd, but he knew better. Looking at a man's library was like looking into his soul. If she realized that, she could learn a lot about him from browsing those shelves.

And he couldn't imagine why in the hell he'd given her the opportunity.

She heard Clint go into the kitchen and slip the chicken into the oven. Since he had a windup timer on his counter, she assumed he set that, too. Browsing the books totally absorbed her. She found it difficult to imagine actually being able to own so many books. Even if she could have afforded to buy so many to begin with, she would have had to leave them behind every time she had to run. And that would have hurt.

She finally found a well-thumbed sci-fi novel, *A Canticle for Leibowitz*. Clearly Clint had read it a good many times, and for some reason the post-apocalyptic setting appealed to her. Distraction, maybe leading to some interesting thinking, especially since Clint seemed to have read it so often.

She returned to the living room to find him absorbed once again in his own book. There was an easy, non-threatening companionship in being able to sit across from him and read. She needed the break.

Most especially she needed the break from her own thoughts. She couldn't bear to remember how much she had wanted to be held by Clint, as if his desire could wash away the stains she felt all over her soul. Stains that had prevented her from taking what he offered. She couldn't bear to think about how broken she was.

But she also couldn't bear to think about the fact that Clint seemed convinced that Kevin would try to get at her here. If Kevin had an ounce of sense, he would have fled far and fast, awaiting some later opportunity to get at her. Keeping her forever living on the edge of fear and always looking over her shoulder.

But Clint didn't seem to think Kevin was going to do that. And Clint knew a lot more about these things, and he had enough confidence in his knowledge to seem certain. In this, she was inclined to trust Clint more than herself. After all, with all Kevin had put her through, she had never, ever thought he would kidnap her.

What was more, when she thought about it, at long last she admitted Kevin might be insane, clinically insane, not just garden-variety crazy. After all, a sane man, someone with even a partial hold on reality, would have left her alone after that prison stint, wouldn't he?

And while it terrified her to think Kevin might come after her again in the next few days, it terrified her less than spending a week here, then moving on to a new place only to discover he'd found her again.

Because despite what Clint said about getting her a new identity, she couldn't believe Kevin wouldn't find her no matter what.

Staring blindly at the page in front of her, she realized that she'd endowed Kevin with both omniscience and omnipotence. Logically, that was ridiculous, but experience insisted otherwise. No matter how carefully she tried to cover her tracks, sooner or later he showed up again. Like some kind of inhuman demon who could track her by scent or something.

Was *she* losing her grip on reality? Did she really think Kevin was something more than just another ordinary, albeit mean, human being?

Horrifyingly enough, that seemed to be exactly the place she'd reached. And logic was a poor answer to experience.

She didn't realize she'd made a sound until Clint spoke. "Something wrong?" he asked.

She hesitated. How much did she want to reveal to this man, who was still basically a stranger she was trusting only because she had to? On the other hand, running around in the circle of her own thoughts wasn't getting her anywhere.

"I just realized that I'm thinking of Kevin as something more than human."

He tilted his head a little. "How so?"

"I've begun to think of him as omniscient. As in, I'll never escape him for long, even with a new identity."

He nodded slowly. "I can understand that."

"No, it's crazy."

He put his book aside. "It's *not* crazy, Kay. Do you know the best way to learn something?"

"How?"

"Through experience. And the more emotionally charged the experience is, the better and more indelibly we learn it." He gave her a smile that was almost bitter. "You're talking to the expert in learning lessons that way."

She bit her lip, fighting back an inexplicable need to soothe him somehow. She knew she wasn't capable of that, but she wished she could anyway.

"So he's followed you from town to town, what? Three times now?"

She nodded.

"I'd begin to wonder if I had a demon on my tail, too."

A relieved sigh escaped her. "That's how it feels."

"Of course that's how it feels. How could it not?"

She couldn't answer, just looked at him, waiting, hoping that somewhere in his educated mind and broadly experienced life he might find an answer for her.

But he surprised her by taking another tack. "I know Kevin," he said.

She gasped and started to curl inward as terror began to wash over her. No, he couldn't! Was this a trap?

"Wait," he said harshly. "I don't mean I know him personally. I mean, I know his type."

She closed her eyes and fought to get her breath back, to still her madly beating heart.

"I'm sorry," Clint said. "Poor choice of words."

"It's okay," she managed. Finally she could breathe again, and her heart rate settled to something approximating normal.

"I'm too used to being alone," he muttered. "I don't put a guard on my thoughts, and now they're spilling out my mouth without due consideration."

"It's okay," she said again. "Damn, Clint, you beat yourself up more than I do."

One corner of his mouth lifted. "Maybe."

She released another long breath, stabilizing emotionally. "You were saying?"

"That I know his type. He's obsessed. That's all it is. He's obsessed enough with you that he wants to control you completely. You got away once when he went to jail. But he found you, only then you got away again. And again."

She nodded. Her eyes felt hot, though she wasn't sure why. God, she was a mess.

"Anyway, he discovered that he enjoyed chasing you. There was fun in finding you after you thought you were safe and then tearing your safety away from you. What he was teaching you was that he *did* control you. No matter how far you ran, or how often."

She gave a jerky nod.

"But this abduction is a new thing, Kay. It means the obsession is changing."

Her heart stopped, then resumed a more rapid beat. "What do you mean?"

"He's tiring of the chase. He's getting bored with the way it was. So this time he took you with him, intending to teach you that he was not only in control of your life, but also your death. He's at a point where he wants to trade you for a new obsession. He's tired of his sport."

"God." She barely breathed the word.

"But he can't get rid of the obsession until he proves his ultimate control and gets rid of you."

"I knew he was going to kill me!" The words burst from her.

"That would be my guess," Clint agreed.

The expression on his face would have terrified her if she hadn't realized by now that it wasn't meant for her. "So he'll come?"

"He'll come. His sickness will drive him to it. He's not going to let you escape. Unfortunately for him, I have other plans."

Chapter 9

The power came back on while they were eating dinner. Kay looked up as she heard the refrigerator compressor kick on.

"Well, that's a good sign," Clint said. But he made no move to turn on the lights, just left the candles they had been using burning.

"Yes," she said. He was probably eager to get back to work. Eager to return to his escape from the world. She couldn't blame him, even though the thought that he might spend hours locked away at his computer while she sat alone in the living room made her feel depressed. Surely she couldn't have become emotionally dependent on him so quickly?

But maybe she had. Once it was clear Kevin would never stop hunting her down, she'd stopped making even loose connections with other people, because she knew that would only add to the pain when she had to run again.

This man had taken her in and offered her safety. Moreover, in more ways than one, he was promising long-term safety. Of course she had started to make a place for him in her heart.

And that was foolish, because she would have to move on again. Even if Clint did manage things so that Kevin could never threaten her again, she couldn't stay here any longer than necessary. Clint wouldn't want it; he was a hermit.

"This chicken is great," he said. "I have to remember your recipe."

"Thanks. It's easy."

He smiled. "Easy is great. And it doesn't make the recipe less worthwhile in the least."

She bit her lower lip, realizing she was doing it again: devaluing herself and her abilities. An overwhelming sense of despair washed over her. Was there any way in which she wasn't broken? And would she ever find the energy or will to put herself back together again? Was it even worth it?

Clint paused, setting his knife and fork down. She looked at him, wondering if he'd heard something, but his ghost-filled gaze was centered on her. Had she made a sound of some kind?

"Was it awful being a foster kid?" he asked out of nowhere.

She sighed. "Sometimes. Not always."

"Meaning?"

"Well, I never felt like I belonged. Being a full-time guest is wearing."

"Did the families make you feel that way?"

"Sometimes. Sometimes they tried really hard to get past that. I was probably a big part of the problem."

"How so?"

"I couldn't feel permanence. Maybe that was because after my grandmother died I was…difficult. Angry, bitter, striking out. So I went through a couple of families fast."

"They didn't expect that kind of stuff? I mean, what were they thinking? You can't take in a kid who's been through the things you have and not expect some adjustment problems."

She shrugged, then winced a little as muscles twinged. "I think some families get into it because if you take in enough kids, you can get a decent chunk of change from the state. Especially if you're careful about how much of that money you actually spend on the kids."

"Ugly," he said flatly.

"People are people. Some better than others." Which was a far more philosophical attitude than she usually had. "So anyway, I was difficult. I admit it. I wasn't suitably grateful, or quiet or willing to accept the way those families thought things should be. I went through three homes in rapid succession because my foster parents couldn't handle me. Or didn't want to. I honestly don't know. I was too young to have any perspective on it."

"Of course you were, which placed a bigger burden on them, and they should have known it."

"I don't know, Clint. For all I know, I was more difficult than most. Anyway, by the time I got to my fourth foster home, I knew I was a trespasser, and that it was just a way station."

"That's sad."

She shrugged again. "It just *was*. I got to the point of existing only to reach adulthood so I could get away and have my own place. It was like suspended animation. I didn't even make friends, because I knew I could be changing schools in just a couple of months."

"That stinks." He said it so harshly that she blinked and stiffened. No, he wasn't mad at her, she realized. She was learning that, finally. About Clint Ardmore, anyway, even if not about the rest of the world.

Something made her continue. "I *thought* that once I was on my own I could put down some kind of roots. I thought I could be normal." She shook her head and looked away. "It didn't happen."

"Tell me." His voice was almost gentle.

"Call it 'child interrupted.' I don't know. I kept trying, but I couldn't believe it. I rented a place, but I barely unpacked. I couldn't even bring myself to hang a picture. I made friends at work, I always had friends. I'd hang out with them, but even so, I look back now and realize there was a part of me I never shared. I never let them really know me, even though when I had to give them up, it hurt. But it didn't hurt as much as it might have if I had let them really close. I was still in suspended animation."

He nodded, his mouth set. "Then Kevin."

"Yeah, then Kevin. The answer to all my prayers." She shook her head and swore softly. "God, I was an idiot."

"Will you please stop saying that?"

"It's true!"

"It's not. It actually makes a ton of sense. So…Kevin. Let me guess. He was warm and friendly and caring, and he made you feel safe. At first."

She closed her eyes. "Yes," she whispered.

"He made you feel as if you'd found an anchor you could really cling to."

"Yes." She dared to open her eyes and look at him.

"And he flattered you, because he was intensely interested in you. In everything about you. He chipped at your walls, and you let him in, because like everyone else on this planet, you were desperate to be cared for."

She nodded, feeling unshed tears burn her eyes.

"You didn't do a damn thing wrong. You were conned."

"Clint…"

"No, you were conned," he repeated. "He could have done the same thing to just about anyone, but you were easier prey than most because of your background. Don't you dare take responsibility for anything Kevin did, because Kevin and his kind are born predators. He used you. That's all on him, and it wouldn't have made any difference who you'd been."

"But…"

He shook his head. "No buts." His eyes grew narrow. "There are people in this world who are born with a gift. They inspire trust, they always seem to know the right thing to say. Some of them use it for good. Others use it to take advantage. And the bad ones…well, their victims are blameless. Don't you see? There's no crime in trusting people to be who and what they say they are. There's no stupidity in that. Most of us start from a position of trust until we find out there's a reason not to trust. This world couldn't function otherwise."

He gave a short, bitter laugh. "I'm probably one of the least trusting people you'll ever meet, but I still trust you. I trust you're telling me the truth. If I didn't, you would have been out of here already."

Her mouth sagged open a bit. "Really?"

"Really. So does that make me an idiot?"

She shook her head slowly.

"See?" He picked up his fork again. "So along comes Kevin, and with a predator's instinct he senses easy prey. Being easy for him doesn't make you stupid, it just makes him meaner."

"Why?"

"Because he could have picked on somebody his size. But he's a freaking coward. Take it from me, lowlifes like him are all cowards. He plays a con game against easy targets, not difficult ones. And he gets his kicks out of it."

She didn't know how to respond to that. It was certainly something she was going to think about.

"So he knew you were already wounded, and he was mean enough to take advantage. Creep."

Almost in spite of herself, she felt a smile tug at the corners of her mouth. "He *is* a creep," she admitted.

"And that's the most printable word I can find for him." He paused, then said, "I rarely make promises, but I'm going to make one now."

"What's that?"

"That I won't rest until Kevin is out of your life for good. Whatever it takes. Prison, a new identity. Hell, I'd probably grin as I was breaking his neck."

Once again she faced the deep well of violence in this man, a well that seemed so contradictory when she thought of how he'd cared for her. She should have been frightened, but apparently some part of her hadn't been totally broken, because she discovered, strangely enough, that she could still trust. One man at least.

"Clint?"

"Yes?"

"I don't want you to do anything that will make you feel worse about yourself."

"Like I'd even notice."

It hurt to hear him say that. "You're a good man."

"You don't know me."

"I know who you are now. Who you've been for the past couple of days. You're a good man. I know you feel bad about things you've done, but they don't define who you are now."

He snorted. "You're one to talk."

"Exactly."

He went perfectly still for a half-minute, then surprised her with a faint smile. "Hoist on my own petard, huh?"

"Maybe. But all the things you've told me to make me feel better about myself? Maybe you should listen to them, too."

He insisted on cleaning up after dinner, telling her to rest.

She sat on the couch, watching him ferry dishes back and forth, then listening to the sound of running water and the clatter as he washed up.

He *was* a good man, she thought. Most emphatically. Bad men didn't feel troubled by conscience. Kevin certainly didn't. She wished there was some way she could make Clint believe that. Psychological mess that she was, though, there was no reason he should listen to her.

She sighed. Then she noticed something else. As the evening deepened, Clint seemed to be coiling tighter in some way. Even when he finished the dishes and returned to his armchair to read, she sensed he was strung as tight as a bow.

"What are you waiting for?" she finally asked him.

"Kevin."

Her heart sputtered, then resumed beating, only faster. "Tonight?" she asked hoarsely.

"Probably not. A predator with an ounce of decent hunting instinct will want to case the place for a couple of days."

"You talk about him as if he's an animal."

"He's worse than an animal. Animals, by and large, hunt because they need to eat, not because they get a charge out of it."

She really couldn't argue with that. "I guess you'd know better about these things than I would."

His gaze darkened. Even in the lamplight she could see the ghosts in his eyes again. She wished she knew a way to exorcise them.

But she couldn't even exorcise her own.

He set his book aside. "Listen, I want to warn you about something."

She tensed. "Yes?"

"I'm going to be wound up tighter than a spring, especially at night. There's no way I can hide it from you. I'm going to be pacing this cabin like a lion in a cage. I'm going to go outside frequently to check things. I just want you to know, because the simple fact that I'm on edge doesn't necessarily mean that I know something is happening right then, okay?"

She nodded slowly, feeling a hollowness inside her.

"I'm going to be hyperalert, hypervigilant. That means... Well, try to avoid startling me, okay?"

"I'll try."

"I'm going to be operating on instincts honed by years of experience in dangerous situations. Unfortunately, that makes *me* dangerous, too."

"I think I understand."

"Maybe you do, to some extent. Maybe not." He shook his head. "I hope you do, because when I react it'll be fast. Thought won't even enter into it."

"Okay." She tried not to let him see that he was making her uneasy. She could get hurt if she startled him? How could she be sure not to do that?

But he seemed to want to move on. "I suggest you take a shower now. Get into some clean clothes. I have more sweats you can wear. Get comfortable. Because later on I'm going to be on guard duty. Speak before you act. That's all I ask."

"I can do that."

The ghosts in his eyes eased a bit. "I know you can."

"But you don't think it'll be tonight?"

He shook his head. "Not tonight. Too soon. He can't be sure how many people are in this cabin. So he'll have to watch. And I'm going to do my damnedest not to scare him off."

Kay took the shower he suggested. It was a relief to be able to get in and out on her own, unlike a bath. The heat of the beating spray helped, too, like a mini massage. Feeling looser all over than she had since Kevin had first beaten her, she dried and dressed in the clean sweat suit Clint had given her. She even managed to comb out her own hair.

The improvement in her ability to take care of herself pleased her, and she was actually smiling when she came out of the bathroom.

Until she realized Clint was gone. Fear gripped her hard, and she backed up against the hallway wall, as if she could press herself right into it. "Clint?"

No answer. What now?

She needed the tire iron. Protection. Slowly she eased down the hallway until she could see the living room. Nobody there, unless someone was hiding on the far side of the couch.

She darted across the room as fast as she could and grabbed her weapon from the couch where it still lay. Then she backed up against the wall again, to ensure nobody could get at her from behind.

Her heart was hammering so hard she was sure it must be audible throughout the entire cabin. She was panting audibly.

She'd always wondered how someone who was terrified could possibly hide. Now she knew—it was impossible.

She gripped the tire iron harder, glad of its weight in her hand. God, where was Clint?

Then she heard the front doorknob rattle and start to turn. At once she shifted her grip, holding the iron bar at the ready in both hands. If Kevin came through that door...

But it wasn't Kevin. It was Clint. He stepped in, locked the door and kicked off his boots. As he was tugging off his jacket, he turned and saw her.

For an instant they both stood locked in a frozen tableau; he astonished, she ready to kill.

Then relief swept through her like a tsunami. The makeshift weapon clattered to the floor, and without a thought for her battered body, her natural inhibitions or anything else except that he was here, she flew across the room and launched herself into his arms.

To her amazement, she didn't bounce off him as if he were a brick wall. Instead he caught her and clutched her close in arms that felt like steel, the best kind of steel in the world.

"It's okay," he whispered. "It's okay. I guess you didn't hear me when I said I was going out."

"I thought...I thought..." She couldn't get the words out. She dug her fingers into his shoulders, then slid her arms around his neck, pressed her face to his shoulder and hid in his strength. *Don't let me go,* she thought desperately. *Please, don't let me go.*

As if he understood, he slipped his arms down until they cradled her bottom. He lifted her high against him, and she wrapped her legs around his waist. If she could have, she would have melted right into him.

"Shh," he said, and only then did she realize she was crying softly, little hiccupping sobs.

"Shh," he said again.

They moved, and the next thing she realized they were sitting on the couch, and she was still wrapped around him like a vine, straddling him and clinging.

His hold shifted as he placed one arm securely around her back and with his other hand held her head close to his own. Cheek to cheek.

"I'm sorry," he said. "I called to you when you were showering."

"I didn't hear." She squeezed the words out.

"God, I'm sorry."

She heard real caring in his tone. Not that he hadn't been caring before, but now there was a note of some kind of recognition. Maybe the recognition of one wounded soul for another. Maybe he'd found a way to liken the demons that drove him to the ones that drove her.

She hardly cared what it was. It was enough that she felt the shared connection between them and knew that he felt it, as well. It had been forever since she'd felt a true connection with anyone. What she'd felt for Kevin had never approached a meeting of hearts. Never.

She leaned against Clint, gradually relaxing into his embrace. For the first time she noticed how good he smelled: of man, soap and fresh air. Intoxicating scents to a woman who hadn't let anyone this close in a long time without the blinding pall of fear in the middle.

Bit by bit the tension seeped from her, and in its place came awareness of other things: his hard, muscled chest; the gentle strength of his hold; his steady breathing near her ear. The aroma of his shampoo. His warmth. How big he was, how powerful. But even that couldn't scare her now, because all that power had devoted itself to protecting her. A godsend.

An amazing godsend, just as she had been about to give up hope.

Then she noticed the heat.

A warmth where their bodies met at the loins as she straddled him. It was as if her attention took a sudden nose dive to her very center, pushing away everything else.

Oh, man, she'd never thought she would feel this way again. Kevin had long since crushed desire out of her, or so she had thought, but here it was, as alive as ever it had been. Acute. Weakening. Demanding an answer.

Two layers of fabric, at least, lay between them, but that only aroused her more. Made her feel safe enough to acknowledge her excitement.

Moist heat. She was spread wide, with her legs on either side of him, and she realized even the slightest movement would brush cloth, and him, against her most sensitive flesh. She held her breath, waiting, waiting, hoping against hope to feel just the slightest brush of fabric as one of them moved. Everything inside her focused on that point of almost-contact.

Oh, please…

Her heart skittered, as if afraid of what she was thinking. She couldn't. She was broken. She would only get so far before she would inevitably frustrate them both. She couldn't do that to him. Not again.

But, oh, how she needed to know that Kevin hadn't utterly destroyed this part of her. Needed to feel hope. Needed Clint. Needed him the way she had needed nothing since her grandmother's death.

She needed him so much it was frightening.

She gasped, drawing a breath finally. And then, hardly moving, afraid to let him know where her mind and body had wandered, because he would have every right to push her away after what she'd done before, she lowered herself the tiniest bit.

Ahh!

Just that little whisper of contact, that little brush of fabric…heaven! Enough to awaken a long-forgotten ache.

"Kay…" he whispered.

No! Please. No. Don't bring back reality. Not now. Not when she was trembling on the lip of a discovery she needed as much as she'd ever needed anything.

His hand slid down her back. Slowly. Carefully. She bit her lip and buried her face in his neck. Hoping. Waiting. *Please take me there!*

His hand reached her bottom, rested there for a few seconds, then gently, oh so gently and carefully, pressed her a tiny bit closer.

A soft groan escaped her as she felt him hard against her, as she realized he wanted her, too. Her fear of being soiled and ugly forever went up in smoke. *He* didn't feel that way about her, and he was letting her know that, letting her know she wasn't alone in this moment of madness.

She pressed her face even harder against his neck, signaling her yearning. Everything deep inside her throbbed now in a way she'd almost forgotten.

She didn't know how to do this, she realized hazily. She didn't know how to reach out for this. She'd never been allowed to. It had always been Kevin who decided, whether she wanted it or not. She had not one bit of knowledge about how to seduce a man.

Nor could she be completely certain she wanted to.

But Clint seemed to understand. Somehow, as if he plucked the thoughts from her very mind, he knew.

The hand on her bottom pushed her a little closer, and another soft groan escaped her. Had anything ever felt this good? Then, driven by an instinct she didn't even know she had, she rocked her hips against him, just once. Just once because she needed something deeper.

"Easy," he whispered.

She almost jerked back as fear spiked in her, but his hand held her close.

"Easy," he whispered. "Slowly. Take your time."

Time was the last thing she wanted to take right now. She was afraid, so afraid, that this moment would suddenly shatter in a burst of fear and self-hatred.

For an instant she thought he was about to push her away, and horror gripped her. But before it could gain control, she realized all he had done was move her a bit. Just a little bit, so there was some space between them. Oh, Lord, he *was* telling her no.

But then he surprised her. His hand slipped between them, between her legs. And with the gentlest of touches, he stroked her through the fabric. Through that layer that not only protected her but seemed to heighten the sensation to a dizzying level.

Oh, heavens, no one had ever touched her that way before. Kevin had always been in a rush, tearing away her clothes to get at what he wanted. This was…this was…

No words would come to her. She lost herself in feeling as Clint's hand continued to stroke her as if she were the most delicate rose petal. Softly. Safely. The guardianship of clothing protecting her from the memories.

Infinitely patient, ever so careful, giving but never taking. Over and over his fingers touched her lightly, until she thought she might go mad from wanting more.

Quiet sounds began to escape her, but she felt safe enough to let them free. The hand on her bottom, the hand between her legs, offered her that freedom in a cushioned, secure place.

Nothing he did caused memories to surface. This was entirely new, entirely different. Helplessly, she gave herself over to his touch. Letting the feelings race through her, carrying her to places she'd never been before. Even when her hips began to helplessly rock, his touch never changed, remaining gentle and sure, giving her freedom to find *herself* again.

Higher she soared, discovering an unexpected joy in opening herself, in surrendering to him and the feelings he evoked.

The ache reached a crescendo close to insanity, but his touch never deepened. Teasing, promising, caring, he took her over the top into an explosion that rocked her to her very core.

She lay boneless and weak against him. His arms cradled her, and the kisses he brushed against her cheek told her she did not need to hide from him. Or from herself.

Finally she found breath to whisper, "I never knew."

"No," he said quietly, "I would imagine you didn't."

He knew her better than she knew herself. Or maybe he just knew Kevin, as he'd said.

But she didn't want to think about Kevin right now, didn't want him intruding on what suddenly seemed to her to be holy ground. She crushed him into the mists of memory, and focused on the here and now.

On the powerful arms that held her so gently. On the big man who had just showed her that she wasn't entirely broken, and had asked not one thing for himself. Not in her wildest imaginings could she have believed a man like Clint existed. Generous. Kind. Undemanding.

But finally one thought wouldn't leave her alone. One thought had to be spoken. "That was selfish of me." She barely got the words past her lips, as shame once again tried to rear its head.

"No," he murmured. "Not at all. You can't imagine the pleasure it gave me."

She lifted her head just enough to see his face. Something there said he wasn't kidding. "But you…"

"Shh," he murmured. "Not every man gets a chance to take a woman to the stars. Especially one who thought she'd never visit them again."

A sigh escaped her, and she let her head fall back to his shoulder. "You took me to the stars," she admitted. "And beyond."

"It's a nice place, isn't it?"

"Wonderful." Then a surprising little imp, long buried, surged in her. "What if I want to go again?"

"I'll gladly be your rocket ship."

Her strength was returning, and she pushed herself up with her hands against his shoulders. At once their loins met again, this time firmly. Oh, she liked that.

"What if…?"

He waited. Then prompted her. "What if?"

She bit her lip and met his gaze from beneath lowered lashes. This was hard to say, but she refused to let herself out of it. She'd been running from too much for too long.

"What if," she said hesitantly, "I want even more?"

A smile began to curve his lips. "Then I'd say I'd love to give it to you."

She almost smiled, but embarrassment overcame her, and she sought refuge again in his neck. "Really?" she asked huskily.

"As much as you want. However you want. But I have a ground rule."

"What's that?"

"We go only where you're comfortable, and we move slowly."

"You'd need the patience of a saint."

"I have plenty of patience. What I absolutely want to avoid is causing you to take any backward steps. You've already had to take enough of those in your life."

She thought about that, then announced, "You're amazing."

"Not really."

"Stop it, Clint. You forget where I've been. I know a good man from a bad one now."

A long breath escaped him, and she almost thought it broke a bit. Concerned, she raised herself upright and looked straight at him. His eyes were closed, hiding his ghosts. Ghosts she wished she could rip out of him with her bare hands.

"Clint?"

"I'll be okay." After a moment he swallowed and opened his eyes. The ghosts were still there, but now something else had joined them. Something warm. Something that made her toes curl.

A few more seconds passed, and then he spoke again. "But there's something I need to do first."

"What's that?"

"I'd be an idiot unworthy of your trust if I didn't take a look outside. It's been an hour."

That long? Fear slammed her again. "But you said it should be several days."

"It should be, and it probably will be. But that doesn't mean I can act on that judgment. There's always the astounding chance I could be wrong."

Despite the return of her fear, she had to smile. He was poking fun at himself, and she liked that. "What if I don't want to let you go?"

"Sorry, lady." Then, with that amazing ease, he lifted her off his lap onto the couch. "First things first. If you haven't changed your mind by the time I get back, we can explore the rocket ship further."

Before he left, he gave her the tire iron again. "Lock the door after me."

Outside, Clint took a few deep breaths of cleansing air. Not because he needed to wash the scent of Kay out of his nostrils, but because he needed to focus single-mindedly on his own prey—Kevin.

The trust Kay had just given him had wrenched those internal cracks even wider; they were beyond hope of cement now. Forever after, even if she left in a few days, those cracks would be filled by Kay.

And he couldn't exactly regret it. The return of feelings other than self-damnation was painful, but it was also good. Maybe he could change.

But first things first, as he'd said. In the garage he had a pair of infrared binoculars. Not the souped-up fancy kind, because he had never needed them, but a basic pair. Just enough to tell him if there was any heat around the tree line.

But first he walked around the house, pretending to check things while keeping an eye out for any movement. He tested the breeze with his nose, like an animal. Years back he'd learned the importance of smells. Your enemy might be on a different diet, which would make him smell different. And in an area like this, which should be empty of anything but animals, even the merest wisp of a human scent of any kind would be important.

Nothing.

He'd cleared the trees back nearly a hundred yards from the house. Not that he disliked trees, but inbred caution from many years on the dangerous side had made it impossible for him to leave cover so close to his home.

As he returned to the garage and picked up the infrared binoculars, he was glad he had been so compulsive. If anything had approached the house tonight, he would be able to tell.

He caught some faint heat signatures from the woods but was pretty sure they were animals. With his regular binoculars he scanned the snow all around and saw no sign of footprints. If Kevin had been watching the place earlier, he hadn't approached the house.

But the absence of sign didn't mean Kevin hadn't been there during the daylight hours to watch. In fact, given what he suspected, he would be willing to bet the man would do his scouting when it was warm—or at least warmer—and clear, even though he would probably save his attack for the middle of the night.

So far everything was okay. But he would have to check again later. Much later, when Kevin would presume the cabin's occupants were soundly asleep.

He returned both pairs of binoculars to the pegs in the garage and made his way back to the front of the house. As he did so, he looked up. The new moon had almost arrived. That would make it a lot harder to see Kevin's approach with regular vision. But it would also daunt Kevin, just a bit, even though the starshine would provide enough light as it magnified itself by bouncing off the snow.

Yeah, Kevin might wait for the cover of the new moon. It would fit, and it would occur about the time Kevin would be getting most anxious to take care of his little mess.

And Clint, despite several years of trying to rein in his impulses toward violence, actually felt a bitter pleasure that the confrontation could not be far off.

Chapter 10

Kay waited for Clint, a morass of emotions. Everything from embarrassment to hope to a new kind of budding fear filled her. She felt so vulnerable right now, and the feeling made her uneasy. Kevin had taught her what it meant to be physically and emotionally vulnerable. Since she had sent him to jail, she'd been busy building protective walls of every kind so that she couldn't be hurt again.

But Clint had slipped past those walls with a delicate touch. She had opened herself to him in a way she had sworn never to do again. If anything, she had opened herself more than ever before, simply because Kevin's approach to sex had always been rough and impatient enough to keep some of her innate barriers in place.

But Clint had slipped past even those. She couldn't help feeling both frightened and exhilarated. Experience and instinct warred inside her, the first warning her not to trust, the second telling her she *needed* to trust. Needed to trust Clint. Needed it for her own survival as a person.

She jumped up when she heard Clint knock on the door. "Clint?" she called when she reached it.

"Just me," he answered.

She opened the door, letting him in with the cold, and watched as he locked it behind him.

"Everything's okay out there," he said immediately. "No sign of him."

Only then did she realize she hadn't been getting wound up only about what had happened between her and Clint. Always, at the back of her mind, no matter how far away he might be, Kevin hovered like a shadow, ever ready to pounce.

"You look cold," she said finally. "Should I make some coffee?"

He paused in the process of kicking off his boots to search her face. For once she could see past the stony facade to the thoughts behind it as clearly as she could look into her own mind. He wondered if she was regretting what they had done.

Was she? Certainty settled in her heart. No. Unable to find another way to respond, she stepped close and hugged him. There was no hesitation in his answering hug. None at all. She was a little amazed, all of a sudden, not just at the barriers she had leaped, but at the barriers he had apparently leaped, as well. When she had met this man, he'd clearly been determined not to let anyone into his life. Yet here she was, if only for a brief time.

He brushed a kiss on the top of her head. "I'll take you up on that coffee," he said huskily.

Slow. He'd said they had to take it slow. Appreciation for him wrapped around her heart. "Okay."

He followed her into the kitchen and helped to make the coffee. While they waited for it to finish, he drew her against his side and held her as he leaned against the counter. Forgetting everything else, even if only for now, she wrapped her arms around his narrow waist and leaned into him. A traitorous thought slipped through her mind; if only she could stay like this forever.

But life didn't offer any forevers, and she knew it. That didn't, however, mean she couldn't pretend for just a few hours or days, whatever time life gave her with him.

They carried their mugs into the living room. This time he didn't take his easy chair but instead sat right beside her on the couch, his arm draped loosely around her shoulders.

Letting her know he was open to her, to being touched, to being hugged. That she didn't have to hide herself or her needs. All at once she felt a glorious sense of freedom unlike anything she had ever felt before. She felt free to be herself without expectation of disapproval.

Tears sprang to her eyes, tears of happiness.

But Clint saw only the tears, not the feeling behind them. "What's wrong?" he asked immediately. "Did I do something?"

"No, no." How could she possibly explain this? "You make me feel...as if it's okay to be me."

A quiet oath escaped him. "Of course it's okay to be you."

"But don't you see?" She looked up at him, tears still hanging on her lashes. "I can't remember ever feeling that way before."

"My God." He whispered the words. "Never?"

"Never. But what about you?" she demanded. "Do you feel it's okay to be you? Have you ever?"

"I used to," he answered after a moment of hesitation. "Maybe I'm working my way back to it. I don't know."

She reached up and palmed his cheek. "It's okay to be you," she said fiercely. "You're a lot more okay than most people."

"You don't know."

"You keep saying that, like I can't see what's right in front of my eyes. You're a born protector. You're kind, generous, thoughtful. Whatever you were before, what you are *now* is the man who's been taking care of a stranger since he found her by the roadside. A man who probably would have been a lot happier not to have his bastion invaded. But you never hesitated. That's the man you are now, Clint, and he's a good man."

His mouth framed a crooked smile. "Maybe."

"No maybe about it." Then she took her newfound courage into her hands and tugged his head a little, just enough to bring him close for a kiss.

She felt him tense, and for an instant she felt a flutter of fear that he would reject her for her forwardness. But when his mouth settled gently onto hers, she realized his tension was because he was controlling himself, trying not to frighten her or bring back bad memories.

"Oh, Clint," she whispered against his mouth. "Oh, Clint." In that instant she would have given anything to heal him the way he was helping her to heal. He didn't deserve the ghosts that haunted him, the demons that he believed lurked within him.

No more, she realized, than she did.

"Easy," he murmured, when she tried to deepen the kiss.

Easy? She was ready to attack him and leap every last wall in one bound. But even as she realized that, she knew he was right. Neither of them knew what might trigger one of the land mines Kevin had planted in her, and she would hate herself if she pulled away again. Because if she did that, he might justifiably never let her this close again.

Patience, she told herself. Patience.

"Are you ready?" he asked huskily.

"Ready?" She pulled back a little, looking at him from heavy-lidded eyes that didn't want to stay open.

"Are you ready to be with me?"

Her heart skipped several beats. For a moment the ugly memories tried to rise, but she beat them down and answered honestly, because he deserved it. "I want to *try.*"

"Then let's explore the rocket ship a little more."

She nodded, waiting, wondering where he would begin.

He began by rising, then lifting her into his arms. "I've never," he said, "been one for making love on a sofa."

Somehow that comment made her want to giggle. "Why not?"

He carried her toward the back of the house. "Something about getting so preoccupied that I'd probably knock us both to the floor."

The giggle escaped her then, and she was glad to see him smile. His gaze met and held hers.

"Do you have any idea," he asked, "just how beautiful and sexy you are?"

She felt her cheeks grow hot and pressed her face to his shoulder. "No," she mumbled.

"Then let me put it this way. I'm having to fight an almost overwhelming urge to behave like an animal in rut. It's been a helluva long time since anyone made me feel this way. You make me hotter than a blacksmith's forge."

"Oh." She liked that. She liked that a lot.

She opened her eyes when he started to lower her feet to the floor.

They were in his bedroom now, dark with night, curtains drawn against the world. The only light came from the hallway behind them.

He had a king-size bed. Well, of course. He was a big man. She only vaguely noticed a dresser, a chair and a doorless closet. The bed gripped her attention, and once again she felt the merest shudder of anticipatory fear.

"We can stop right here," he said, as if he read the fear on her face.

She looked at him. "Right now all I'm afraid of is disappointing you."

"That's impossible," he said flatly.

"How can you know that?"

"Because the only thing that would disappoint me right now is myself, if I do something stupid and scare you."

"I'm not worried about that." Well, only a little. Realizing he wouldn't carry her any farther because he needed to know this was her own choice, she walked over to the bed on rubbery knees and lay down.

A moment later he joined her, reaching out for her hand and clasping it. Minutes ticked by as they remained like that, looking up at the ceiling.

"When is launch time?" she asked finally.

A chuckle escaped him. "That's up to you."

"Hmm. What if I said I don't know how to…launch?" It embarrassed her to admit it, but she sensed that truthfulness was the only thing that would serve both of them right now.

"Do you want me to lead?" he asked.

She rolled onto her side and looked at him. "I never had a choice," she said. "I might as well have been a plastic doll with Kevin, and there's never been anyone else."

"Son of a bitch," he said, though his tone was mild enough.

"Yeah, he was."

"Not supposed to be that way." Now he rolled onto his own side to face her, leaving only a few inches between them. He propped his head on his hand so he looked down at her. "Wanna play a game?"

"What kind of game?"

"Let's pretend you've never done this before. Any of it. This is your very first time."

She swallowed and nodded. That might be hard. But the idea held a certain appeal. "Okay."

"And let's pretend I'm the big bad seducer of young maidens who have no experience."

"I don't know about the bad part."

He shrugged a little. "Most people might think a seducer is bad."

"But what if I need one?"

"Then maybe it's not bad at all." He reached out to brush her cheek gently, to push her hair back. Then he traced the outline of her ear with his finger, and a shiver of longing ran through her.

"Just make me one promise," he said.

"If I can."

"Tell me if I do anything you don't like for any reason at all. You don't have to explain a thing. Just say no, okay?"

She nodded and swallowed again. Her heart had begun to beat heavily and her breathing accelerated. "I promise."

"Good." He smiled a little and ran his finger around the shell of her ear once more, before letting it trail down to the pulse in her neck. A soft gasp of pleasure escaped her, as sparks seemed to run from his fingertip to her center.

"See?" he murmured. "This can be a fun game."

"Have you played it before?"

"I never needed to before. But I think I'm going to like it a whole lot."

She thought she would, too.

"Close your eyes, darlin'," he said quietly. "Just feel."

And oh, he made it so easy to do exactly that. She lay there, her breathing growing quicker as he continued to stroke her face and throat. Deep inside a different kind of pounding began, a pounding that wanted answers.

Answers he didn't give. He continued to stroke her ear and throat until she found her whole body willing him to touch her elsewhere, anywhere, because instinct and need demanded more.

But he was patient, maybe too patient. Even so, she was afraid to rush him as he slowly and surely carried her into a whole new world of hunger and beauty.

"Easy now," he murmured, almost a warning, and then his hand left her throat. Slowly it swept downward, along her side to her hip, then back up again. He repeated the movement until a long shaky sigh escaped her and her body, of its own accord, tried to move closer.

"Easy," he said again. "Just enjoy the feelings. We have plenty of time."

But it was so hard. He'd barely touched her, really, yet he'd awakened so many feelings that she had thought were lost to her forever. Never had she imagined that passivity could be so difficult. With Kevin she had frozen inside, allowing herself to feel nothing at all as she did exactly as he asked.

This man was asking nothing, and he was unfreezing her. Fast.

"Clint," she whispered.

"A little more?" He obliged before she could answer. His hand stopped wandering her side and brushed over one breast. The electric shock was so sudden and unexpected that she arched and gasped.

"Oh, that's nice, isn't it?" he said, his voice throaty. "Very nice. You have beautiful breasts, you know."

Did she? Hazily she remembered Kevin thinking they were too small and complaining about it. But Kevin wasn't here. Not in this place. And Clint seemed to think something else entirely.

"See," he murmured, closing his hand around her. "You fit perfectly in my hand." Then his thumb rubbed over her nipple through the fabric, and a moan escaped her. "Perfect," he murmured. "So perfect I want to kiss it."

"Yes," she whispered. "Yes." Oh, please, yes.

His hand dipped down, sliding across her belly, striking more fire, and as it moved upward again it slipped under the sweatshirt. She gasped, loving the feel of his callused palm against the soft skin of her midriff. Loving how it scratched ever so slightly as it moved tantalizingly upward. Slowly upward. Giving her ample time to object.

But objection was the last thing on her mind.

Now his hand cupped her breast without the fabric barrier, and without a thought she pressed herself harder into his palm. This was what she wanted. This was what she had never known.

His thumb brushed back and forth, teasing, taunting, satisfying and dissatisfying all at once. And then she felt the merest breath of cool air before his tongue replaced his thumb. He flicked her nipple, cool and swollen, with wet heat until a small groan escaped her and she tried to reach for him.

"Shh," he said. "I'm nowhere near done seducing you."

At that moment she would have said she didn't need any more seduction. Already she was getting close to the stars he'd shown her for the first time just a short while ago.

Then she jerked in astonishment and relief as his mouth closed over her nipple. He sucked gently on her at first, then more strongly, until it seemed there was a direct line between his mouth and the point of sensation between her legs. Her whole body throbbed in time with his mouth, and her legs loosened, then tightened, as she tried to find relief.

"You are so sweet," he whispered. Then his mouth moved to her other breast, giving her attention she had barely realized she needed.

"Clint," she moaned, getting more impatient by the second. Yet he would not hurry, not even when she grabbed his shoulders and tried to pull him closer.

"Not yet," he said softly. "I want you over the moon with me."

He was going over the moon? Something in her healed over in an instant. Another wordless moan escaped her as her body took over, rocking her hips, seeking more and still more.

A little laugh escaped him, as if he were pleased. Then, as he continued to tongue her nipple and suck her breast, his hand slipped down along her hip and back to the place it had touched before. Still outside the fabric, shielding her from intimacies that might come too soon. And again he stroked her as if she were the most delicate flower.

She was caught, strung on a wire of fire running from her breast to her core. Her body shivered and struggled toward the stars, but he wouldn't quite let her go there.

Almost, but not quite. Who would have thought torture could be so wonderful?

"Clint…"

"Are you really ready, darlin'?"

Her eyes flew open and looked straight into his. "I've never been this ready in my life."

He chuckled softly. "Be sure. Very sure."

She had no doubts, not even when she felt him begin to tug the sweatpants down. She even lifted her hips to help, glad to be rid of them.

Then his fingers found her petals, and the pleasure-pain sensation was so exquisite that a cry escaped her.

He stopped at once. "Are you all right?"

"Oh, please, don't stop!" Past all thought and reason, she knew what she wanted. She reached for his shirt with one hand, his belt with the other. "Clint..."

"Easy." He rolled away briefly, and when he came back to her, he was nude. In the dark she could see very little, but at last she could touch him, learn him, try to make him half as crazy as he had made her.

He pulled the sweatshirt over her head, the sweatpants from around her ankles, then tugged her close so they met, skin on skin from breast to thigh. She felt his hardness against her and threw her leg over his hip, wanting that hardness inside her as she'd never wanted anything in her life.

She felt him press against her, an answer but not enough. Instead his hands and mouth continued to roam her body, as if he wanted to memorize every silky inch.

"Anything you want," he murmured just before he kissed her mouth. "Anything. Just let me know."

She wrapped her arms as tightly around his neck as she could and thrust her hips against his. "I want *you*."

No doubt, no question. He'd carried her to the point of no return.

"Then hang on just a second." He rolled away, and she heard what sounded like a drawer, then something tore. A familiar scent assailed her nostrils, and for an instant, just an instant, she remembered another time. Another first time when simple precautions had struck her as caring. She froze.

But then he came back to her, and before she could become totally locked in memory, he began again to caress her in those amazing ways, ways that took her so far out of herself that she was in a universe where Kevin had never existed.

"Clint, please," she begged, her voice thick with need. "Please. Now." She didn't think she could bear another minute of this exquisite torture.

He surprised her. He didn't push her onto her back. No, he lifted her so that she straddled him and had to brace her hands on his shoulders. He held her waist, stilling her.

"As much as you want, no more," he said, his own voice husky with passion. "You're in charge. You lead the way."

She knew exactly where she was going now. She positioned him with her hand, feeling the latex, accepting that he cared enough to protect her, wishing he didn't have to, and then she lowered herself.

Slowly. He was big. So very big, and her muscles stretched as if this was the very first time for her. That, too, made it special, seeming almost to cleanse the stains on her spirit.

Certainly it was her first time with Clint. And she reveled in it.

She took him slowly, but once he was fully within her, a sigh of sheer pleasure escaped her. Then, with his hands on her hips, it was she who took them both to the stars.

"I need to take care of something," he murmured in her ear.

She lay hot, sweaty and utterly sated atop him. "No." The last thing on earth she wanted was to be separated from him by even so much as an inch.

"Yes," he said, and there seemed to be humor in his voice. "I don't want to give you an unexpected present."

She sighed, letting him reach between them to remove himself cautiously from her hot, wet depths, then allowed herself to be rolled gently to the side.

"I'll be right back," he said, and showered a few kisses on her face and breasts.

She didn't want to move. Not one single muscle. She didn't want to lose one bit of what she was feeling right now.

Eyes closed, she listened to Clint go into the bathroom, listened to the water run, and sensed the exact instant he returned to the room. How had she lived so long and never realized it could be like this?

He lifted her, surprising her eyes open, then put her back down, this time on a sheet. He pulled the covers over her, then slipped under them with her and drew her close. She snuggled into him, into the safe haven he had made for her.

And finally she said, "That was some rocket ride."

A quiet laugh escaped him. "I've never had a better one. Ever."

Moments she never wanted to end stretched before her in a golden glow. The transformation inside her seemed almost impossible to believe, yet there it was. She had changed. Forever.

The phone rang. This time it was Clint who groaned. "Hell," he said.

She felt the same, but only for an instant. *Kevin.* It had to be about Kevin. With one ring of the phone he came slamming back into her world. Her heart skittered, and every muscle in her body coiled.

And this time Clint didn't tell her to relax. Even in the dim light from the hallway, she saw the return of the stone mask.

He hurried out to get the phone, which was in the living room. She could only hear the sound of his voice, not the words. She lay stiff and waiting, afraid of what he might be learning. She squeezed her eyes shut and hoped it was just an old friend, nothing about Kevin.

But even so, Kevin had returned to her mind, with all the terror he had taught her. She couldn't banish him. She might never be able to banish him.

"Kay."

She opened her eyes and saw Clint in the doorway. He was still naked.

"Get dressed," he said. "I'm not going to turn on the light in here. Can you see well enough?"

"What's going on?"

"Just get dressed. I got the mud off your shoes earlier while you dozed, so your feet will be protected."

Terror rose in her as Clint grabbed his clothes from the floor and disappeared while she scrambled into the sweat suit. The socks he had loaned her lay on the floor, forgotten. They wouldn't fit inside her jogging shoes anyway.

Her legs felt like lead as she went to the living room. There she saw something that made her freeze and gasp.

Clint was standing there, snapping his jeans, his back to her as he jammed his feet into his boots. But what she saw on his back gave a whole new meaning to "wounded." Burn scars, deep dips in the flesh that suggested he had been shot and might even be missing parts of himself.

He heard her gasp, and he turned. More scars on his belly. Old ones. How had she not felt those scars with her hands?

He saw where she was looking. "Sorry," he said roughly. "I know it's not pretty."

Her mouth felt dry, but she found her voice. "It's the pain, not how it looks. God, you must have suffered."

"Morphine is a wonderful thing." But he was hurriedly reaching for his shirt, trying to hide the scars from view.

She wouldn't let him. To hell with Kevin. She crossed the room fast, before he could button his shirt, and reached out with both hands, pressing them to his belly, then sliding them around to trace the scars on his back.

"Don't hide from me," she whispered, tightening her hold and pressing her face to his chest. "Please don't."

He stilled and let her hands trace the old scars. Then a sigh escaped him. "Kay, I need to recon. Now."

She lifted her face and looked up at him. "You're beautiful, you know. You really are."

Something in his expression shifted, but only briefly. The stone returned hard and fast. "I've got things to do," he said.

She didn't know if he was trying to escape her, silence her, or simply reacting to the pressure, but regardless, she stepped back and let him finish dressing.

"Your shoes are in the den," he said. "They should be dry by now."

"Okay."

"Keep the door locked. And grab that tire iron."

"What happened?"

He paused halfway to the door and looked back. "Kevin was seen in town today. The sheriff has been showing his mug shot around, and apparently a merchant ID'd him."

"Oh God! He'll hear they're looking for him."

He shook his head. "Not in this county. People might talk among themselves, but they never gossip with strangers—*any* strangers—and especially not about something like this."

He started toward the door again. "Lock up after me," he reminded her. "And finish dressing."

She did as she was told, trying to keep a handle on her fear. She wasn't alone this time. She had Clint. And Clint would, by any measure, be more than Kevin could handle.

But that didn't keep her from picking up the tire iron after she tied her shoes.

The wait seemed endless, but at last there was a knock at the door.

"It's me," said Clint.

She opened the door and let him in. She wanted to throw herself into his arms, let him hold her and drive away the terror once again, but something about him made her pause. She watched as he locked the door, then shed his coat and boots.

"Did you see anything?"

"Not yet."

He walked past her, and she noted the shift in him. He was no longer the lover who had been so gentle. Now he moved like a large cat coiled to spring at any moment. It was almost a relief when he knelt before the fire and put another couple of logs on. That at least seemed normal and ordinary.

But the ghosts were back. She saw them the instant he straightened and faced her.

"You can relax for now," he said. But the gentleness was gone from his voice, and his eyes had a distant look to them. As if he were focused somewhere else.

"Maybe," she said hesitantly, "you should call the cops to come get me. Or take me to them yourself."

Now his gaze snapped into focus, and she knew for certain he saw her. "Why do you say that? You were dead set against it."

"Because I'll never forgive myself if something happens to you. Or if you have to do something you'll regret later. I've been selfish. So selfish."

"No."

No? She stared back in astonishment. "No?"

He shook his head. "This ends soon, and it ends here. If I take you to the cops, there's no telling when that bastard will find you again. No. This time it's *my* way."

Before she could begin to muster an argument, he started to move. Window by window he removed the obstacles he'd laid out.

"Why are you doing that?"

"I only put them there so you could sleep easily. So you wouldn't be lying awake in terror that he might get in while you slept. They're not necessary."

"No? Then how the hell will you know if he breaks in?"

The smile he gave her was chilling. "I'll know. I'll know as soon as he makes the attempt. And the last thing I want to do is scare him off."

She didn't know if she liked this, but he seemed so certain.

"You only need a perimeter warning system when you don't have enough sentries to cover the entire perimeter," he said, as if trying to get her to understand. "You have a sentry. Me. Just trust me on this, Kay. The bastard is counting his freedom in days now, if not hours."

She certainly hoped he was right about that. But Kevin had taken on such monstrous proportions in her mind that he seemed superhuman.

But then, Clint was taking on those proportions now, too, and for a much better reason. Finally she sagged onto the couch, still holding the tire iron, and let him do whatever he thought necessary.

Because Clint was right about one thing, if nothing else, this had to end. Over the last few days, Clint had taught her so much about the kind of life she wanted to have, a kind of life that was actually possible if she could get out from under Kevin's shadow for good.

And she couldn't think of a better reason than that to make the stand here and now.

Clint finished up at the back of the house. When he returned, though, he took his easy chair instead of sitting beside her, and she ached, feeling dismissed.

Yet some part of her realized that wasn't fair. He had gone into some kind of mode that precluded distractions. He had the look of a hunter, she thought, and it wouldn't be wise to break that concentration.

She ought to know. Intense focus had saved her more than once.

"Kay?" His quiet voice pierced a silence that had been punctuated only by the crackle of the fire for what seemed a long time now.

"Yes?"

"I want you to know…" He hesitated.

She waited, sensing he was struggling with something. No point in pushing him.

He tried again. "The part of me you'll see until we get Kevin...*you* don't need to fear it."

"I know that." Her own certainty came as a surprise.

"Do you?" He searched her face. "But some of it may...horrify you."

"After what I've been through? For the love of God, Clint, I've been beaten, burned, kicked, raped, strangled, kidnapped, starved and pursued across half the country. Maybe there haven't been any guns or bullets yet, but I have a nodding acquaintance with what men are capable of."

"I guess you do." His face darkened.

"So let's be clear on something I've finally figured out."

"What's that?"

"That sometimes, just sometimes, it matters *why* people do bad things. And self-defense, or the defense of another, seems like the best reason anyone could have."

One corner of his mouth lifted. "Well, that's Just War Theory in a nutshell."

The remark came at her sideways, but then she caught his reference. "Really? I came up with something that smart on my own?"

He shook his head and sighed. "When are you ever going to believe you're not stupid? You don't need a wall full of degrees to be smart, Kay. Believe me. You're smart."

"I'd still like the degree."

"When this is over, we'll make that dream come true. God knows, you have everything it takes to get the piece of paper."

That lit a little warm glow in her heart. But there was a bridge to be crossed first. A scary bridge.

"So," she said hesitantly, "what's the plan? What do we do?"

"We wait." His gaze grew distant again. "I don't think he'll come tonight. It's too soon after the blizzard. He couldn't have scouted enough to be sure how many people are in the house."

"Tomorrow night?"

"Possibly. If I were him, I'd wait for the dark of the moon, but he doesn't have my training. My guess, and it's only a guess, is that he'll want another day to make sure there are only two of us here."

"And then?"

"And then he'll come when he's sure we'll be asleep. I'm betting somewhere between two and four in the morning."

"But we won't be asleep."

"No way."

She nodded, compressing her lips. "That sounds right," she said after a few moments of thought. "He used to come after me at night, when he hunted me down. Twice he caught me in bed asleep. The last time…well, I was out jogging. Some of those country roads can be pretty empty. I thought I'd be safe because I'd hear any cars coming."

"But you weren't?"

She shook her head. "Obviously. He was waiting for me, not following me. He jumped out from behind some bushes and hit me on the head before I realized what was happening."

"Hell." He met her eyes. "Let's get something clear right now."

"What's that?"

"You saw that my only closet doesn't have doors. So when I tell you to hide, you get under the bed. No ifs, ands or buts."

"Why?"

"Because there are two of us in this house, and he's going to know it. Because he wants to end this. My guess is he's going to come armed with something more than a tire iron or a knife."

"Oh my God." She breathed the words. "Clint, you've got to take me to the police. I don't want you to risk your life!"

"No," he said, stone-faced and impassive.

"Dammit, don't give me that Sphinx crap! If he shoots you…" Oh, God, she couldn't bear to even think about it.

"First of all," he said levelly, "Kevin isn't going to know I'm waiting for him. Secondly, I have body armor, a relic from the past. I just wish I had some for you. So you're going to get under the bed, right?"

She nodded. "If there's time."

"There's going to be time. That's where you're going to be *before* he gets into this house."

"How can you know that?"

"Because I'm going to be awake and waiting."

It sounded like a Möbius strip of thoughts to her, but he seemed so self-assured that she couldn t doubt him.

Helplessly, she looked at the pendulum clock ticking on the mantelpiece. It was the first time she had honestly cared what time it was, but now that clock had become all-important.

Because she knew he was right. Kevin would come in the dead of night. The only question was which night.

At midnight Clint went outside again. Ten minutes later he was back with an odd-looking pair of binoculars. "Night vision," he said shortly when she looked curious.

Then he walked through the house, turning out the lights one after another, until the glow of the flickering fire was the only illumination. The shadows grew deep, moving as if with a life of their own.

He had begun to pace in deadly earnest now, moving from room to room with surprising silence.

She watched him, growing increasingly on edge, wishing for distraction but knowing it would be dangerous now.

"Damn fire," he muttered at one point.

"What's wrong with it?"

"I can't look out the front windows. If I pull the curtains back even a bit, he could see, because there would be light behind me."

"Can we put it out?"

He shook his head. "No central heat. Besides, I might as well send up a flare, letting him know we're on the lookout."

He paused, obviously thinking. "Okay, I'm fairly certain he won't come from the front. He might be seen.

Sarah said they're increasing road patrols in this area. Not heavily, but enough. He won't be familiar with the usual patrol patterns, so it shouldn't alert him."

She nodded, trying to follow.

"No, he'll want maximum cover. That means the back."

"And you nailed the windows shut," she reminded him.

He shrugged. "That was mostly for you. Breaking a window would announce his arrival, and sliding one open makes noise, especially with wood frames. And then it takes time to climb through, time when he'd be exposed. No, he's going to try to jimmy a door lock. Maybe pick it." He looked at her. "You think he knows how to pick a lock?"

"Probably. He got into my apartment twice without alerting the neighbors. Afterward, there was no sign of damage to the locks."

"Good." His smile was unpleasant. "He'll be counting on that, then."

He paced through the house once more, then glanced at the clock. It was almost one. "In a little while I'm going to ask you to move to the bedroom. If anything happens, anything at all, promise you'll get under that bed."

When she looked as if she might object, he went on.

"Look," he said sternly, "I don't want to have to worry about you. I want you safely out of the way so I can do my job."

"Okay." But she rebelled at him taking risks for her, though the more reasonable part of her knew she wasn't capable of handling this on her own. Experience had taught her that. No matter how she had fought, Kevin had always gotten the upper hand, until finally she had learned not to fight at all. But one thing she was sure of, although she didn't tell him, and that was that she would not simply hide. Not anymore. If she didn't fight for herself, she would lose something essential and never be able to get it back.

She sighed. Then something else rose to the forefront of her mind. "How were you wounded?"

For several seconds he didn't answer. "Which time?"

Her mind balked. "More than once?"

"More than once," he agreed. "Let's see. Shrapnel and burns from a roadside bomb. A bullet from a sniper. A knife in the back during a covert op."

"But didn't you have armor?"

"When you're undercover, armor could give you away."

"Oh." Her heart squeezed. "So how many parts did you lose?"

"None that matter. Spleen, a chunk of lung, part of a rib, some bits of muscle. Nothing I can whine about."

She hated to imagine what *would* make him whine. "Does it still hurt?"

"Sometimes. Old injuries do that, even when you get them from basketball or soccer."

Feeling her own dulling aches and pains, she could only marvel at his acceptance. "How do you make yourself go back after something like that?"

"Go back to the job, you mean?"

She nodded.

"The same way you're making yourself face this mess right now. Because you have to."

She could see a commonality in that, although there was a huge different in degree.

"And we need to be quiet now," he said. "Our voices could be heard."

Fear slammed her again, but this time she forced it down. When he offered his hand, she took it, and allowed him to lead her back to the darkened bedroom.

"You can sit on the chair or lie on the bed," he murmured. "Just stay awake so you hear me if I tell you to hide."

"I don't think anything could make me sleep right now." And she didn't. Adrenaline and fear were coursing through her so powerfully that she was sure even lying down would be impossible. She found her way to the chair and sat, wondering if even that would drive her crazy.

Clint pulled off his socks and resumed his prowling on silent bare feet. At first she wondered at that, then realized he didn't want to slip on his socks. At one point, as he passed the bedroom door, she saw that his dark silhouette had changed, had grown bulkier. No doubt the body armor he'd mentioned earlier.

Rarely had a few hours seemed to drag by so slowly, and every time they had, it had always been bad. Why couldn't time slow down when things were wonderful, like when they'd made love earlier? Why did those moments seem to slip by so quickly?

Her thoughts wanted to return to that interlude, to relive it again and again, holding it up as assurance that life could be beautiful, that she could be whole again. Finally she just gave in and let it, while her eyes watched the red numbers on the digital alarm by the bed change minute by minute.

Clint was an amazing lover, and she didn't need a whole lot of experience to tell her that. Her body recognized it as surely as if her experience had come with a million testimonials. Maybe better.

He'd awakened feelings so long dormant she'd begun to believe they had died. And now she knew one thing for certain—she wanted to live long enough to make love with Clint again.

If that meant sitting here in the dark, terrorized by a memory and a threat, then she would do it. She shifted her hold on the tire iron, cherishing the bit of protection it offered, but cherishing more the man who prowled the house like a giant cat, on guard and ready.

After years of running and hiding, she'd found someone who was willing to stand up for her, willing to stand *with* her, even at huge risk to himself. Someone who hadn't even wanted her here in the first place, but had a huge enough sense of duty and honor to care for her anyway.

How many places could you find a man like that? Very few, as well she knew. She'd faced impatient prosecutors, impatient cops, people who thought they had much more important things to deal with. People who cared, but not enough, who were perhaps too busy to care. When they told her they didn't have enough evidence, she'd wondered if she was somehow supposed to provide more than her own battered, abused body as proof. But Kevin, all but that one time, had had an alibi. And he'd left nothing behind to betray him.

She'd especially hated it when they had been hinted that maybe *she* was somehow letting Kevin know how to find her. That maybe *she* got some sick pleasure out of the horror of her own life.

Her hands tightened so hard on her weapon that she had to force them to relax before they started to weaken.

Then came the dawn, and with it the sickening realization that she still had to look forward to the threat and another night of endless tension.

God, she wanted to be sick.

"Get some sleep," Clint said from the doorway. "I'm good for a few more hours, but then I'm going to need you to spell me."

She would have liked to ask him to sleep with her, to feel the security of him wrapped around her, but she understood his concern. Everything had to give way to vigilance now.

Unless the cops found him. But Kevin was smarter than that. He'd already proved that several times over.

Clint was right; Kevin would come at night, and he would come from the rear. He would come from where he was sure nobody could see him.

Because while he might be crazy, he wasn't stupid.

She put down the tire iron and crawled into the bed. She could still smell the musky scent of their lovemaking, and it soothed her somehow. At last she found forgetfulness in sleep.

Chapter 11

He woke her around noon with coffee. Sitting on the edge of the bed, he called her name quietly until her eyes fluttered open.

Even though he tried to mask it with a smile, she could see weariness in his face.

"You shouldn't have let me sleep so long!" At once she sat up and tried to swing her legs to the floor, but he was in the way.

He was still smiling when he reached out to touch her legs. A gentle, tentative touch. She felt warmth run through her like syrup.

"My turn to sleep," he told her. "Do you want your coffee here, or would you be more comfortable elsewhere?"

What she wanted was to grab him and drag him down onto the bed with her. Without the guardian of full wakefulness, desire rose up like a tidal wave. She could feel her cheeks heat.

"What I want," she managed to say, "isn't on the menu this morning."

At that a quiet chuckle escaped him. "At least not right now." His eyes held a warmth she'd almost never seen there.

"So everything's okay?"

"So far."

She decided she had to get out of the bed or everything was *not* going to be okay. With the way he had distracted her yesterday, she was quite certain that if they went there again, Kevin would be able to bash his way into the house and she would never even hear him.

With a reluctant sigh, she climbed out of the warm bed and padded into the front room.

"Breakfast, too?" she asked as she emerged from the hallway and saw the table.

"Hot and ready," he said.

She almost giggled at his choice of words, even though he probably hadn't meant them as a double entendre. But when she stole a glance at him, she amended her judgment. Maybe he *had* meant them that way.

A touch of shyness overcame her then, enough to get her to the table and seated before a plate of steak and eggs. "This looks wonderful!"

"I was surprised you didn't wake up while I was cooking."

"Now that I see what you've been up to, I'm surprised, too."

Her own hunger also surprised her, and while he'd served her far more than she would have chosen on her own, she devoured a surprising amount of it. They didn't talk much as they ate, but what were they going to talk about?

Not their lovemaking, not now. Not Kevin, because he couldn't be allowed to ruin this meal. Not the future, because right now neither of them was sure if they had one, or what it might be. But somehow the silence that had initially been a regular part of this household now seemed uncomfortable.

Too much on their minds, she decided. Too many subjects to avoid. And she found herself actually hoping that Kevin would come that night. She wanted this over with.

At last he finished. "Wake me at four," he said.

She looked at him. "Will that be enough sleep for you?"

"Absolutely. And I want to be wide-awake before it gets too dark." He paused. "Look out the windows from time to time. Just don't get too close to them."

She nodded, suppressing a shiver as the darkness moved into her mind again. She watched him disappear down the hall, then, moving slowly because the bruises still ached and some new aches had been added by their unexpected lovemaking, she cleared up and washed the dishes. It kept her busy.

She looked out all the windows, copying what she had seen him do, barely twitching curtains aside so she could see the empty areas around the house. No sign of danger that she could see.

When she went back to the couch at last, she found a surprise waiting for her, a thick hardcover book. There was no jacket, but the cover was dull green, and stamped into it in black were the title and author: *Just War Theory: a Survey and Reflections*. Below the title, in smaller print: Clint Ardmore, PhD. USMC (Ret.).

His book!

She sat and eagerly opened it. When she got to the flyleaf, her breath caught and her throat tightened.

Kay, he'd written in a bold hand, *you understand far better than you know. Clint.*

She stared at the words, feeling a throb in her chest. Nobody had ever given her a gift like this, a gift that said she was bright enough to understand.

She clutched the book to her breasts and closed her eyes for a minute, hugging the feelings, hugging the intent, wishing she could hug Clint right this minute.

Then, cautiously, sure she wouldn't begin to understand this kind of book or even this kind of writing, she opened to the preface and began to read.

Much to her surprise, she was drawn right in.

Hours later she looked up to realize that the day was darkening. A glance at the clock caused her heart to skip.

He'd said four. It was already four-thirty. Where had the time gone?

She put the book aside and jumped to her feet. She hurried back to the bedroom, aware that night was already beginning to encroach. She hoped he wouldn't be angry with her.

"Clint?"

He sprang out of bed as if launched and settled into a crouch.

"Clint, it's me."

Slowly he relaxed and straightened. The first words he spoke were, "It's getting dark."

"I know. I'm sorry. I was reading your book and lost track of time. Don't be mad at me." She was already tensing, moving backward, shaking.

"Why the hell would I be mad at you?" It was almost a bark, making her jump back farther. "Kay..." He adjusted his tone. "I'm sorry," he said quietly. "I'm not mad at you. I can't imagine ever being mad at you. I was just startled."

She began to breathe again, although she still felt shaky. "Because I was late getting you?"

He shook his head. "If things like that made me mad, I'd be nuts."

"Or Kevin," she admitted.

He swore quietly. "I'm sorry. What you just saw was my own demon at work. I still wake up as if I'm under attack."

"I know what you mean."

He nodded. "I think you do."

She hesitated. "Thank you so much for the book. I'm enjoying it."

"You're just saying that to be nice. It's as dry as bones."

She shook her head. "No. I really am enjoying it. It's slow reading, but I'm learning a whole lot. That's why I woke you late. I got absorbed."

"Well." He sounded almost pleased. "That's really nice to hear. People say it about my novels, but I think you're the first person, other than a professor or two, to actually say that about the textbook."

"Well, I'm certainly not a professor."

"Wouldn't surprise me if you took that route someday." Evidently deciding they'd both relaxed enough by now, he approached her and slowly slipped his arms around her. "I need my head examined," he said almost to himself, then bent to kiss her.

She sailed away again to a far planet, a place where nothing existed except Clint. And she would very much have liked to stay there, except just as she started to wind her arms around him, he broke the kiss.

"Damn," he said almost ruefully. "I gotta get rid of that guy. He's interfering with my desire to sweep you off your feet and right into my bed."

She felt a current of joy mixed with desire zap through her. "Really?"

"Really," he admitted. "But first things first. I want the bastard off my plate. And off yours. Then we'll have time to decide if we both just went temporarily insane."

Well, Kay thought as they headed to the front of the house, that was always possible. If so, she wanted to go permanently insane.

But the shadows were deepening, and with them her fear. She wondered if she would ever feel truly comfortable in the dark again.

But Clint surprised her. He headed straight for the kitchen, turned on a few lights, and asked her if peanut butter sandwiches were okay with her.

"Sure." She hesitated. "Um… Why did you turn on the light?"

"Because we've got to make it look normal in here. It's supper time. Lights in the kitchen. Go turn on a light or two in the living room."

"We want him to think we don't expect anything?"

"You got it." He flashed her a smile, though only a small one.

"Are you going outside to look again?"

"Not tonight."

"Why not?"

"Because if he's been watching, he knows I've been on alert. I want him to think I'm asleep at the wheel now, feeling safe."

She had never imagined how much psychology went into this sort of thing. "Have you been planning this all along?"

"Lady, that's what they used to *pay* me to do."

She was still standing on the kitchen threshold. Questions kept bubbling up. "But…"

He raised a hand. "Give me five to make sandwiches. Then we'll talk about what I've been doing, and why I'm changing the pattern now."

"Okay." She could agree to that. She went and turned on a few lights, signaling even through the curtains that the people inside the cabin were up and about and busy.

She would have felt safer with less light, despite her fear of the shadows, but she trusted Clint to know what to do.

And that brought her up short. She trusted Clint a whole lot, she realized. She trusted him completely. Was that wise? Her heart said it was.

They ate their sandwiches at the table, accompanied by tall glasses of milk.

"Okay," he said. "I've been listening to you and building a picture of Kevin in my head. A profile. I think I know what he's thinking and what will draw him in."

She nodded. "Okay."

"I realize you know him better, but I know predators, obsessives and bastards. I'll allow I could be wrong, but I don't think so."

She nodded. "Go on."

"I've been keeping an eye out in part to catch some sign of him. The need for that evaporated yesterday when Sarah called to say he'd been spotted in town. Whether or not I catch sight of him in the woods now is irrelevant. He hasn't run away to try again another day. He's here, and there's only one reason for that—he knows you're still around."

She nodded, and peanut butter suddenly stuck in throat. She reached for her milk and took a few swallows, wishing she could be anywhere near as clinical about this as he was.

"Am I disturbing you? Upsetting you too much?"

"No," she said. "Well, yes, but I want to know. I've got to know."

He nodded, measuring her. "Okay. We know he's out there. So he's going to come. If he's watched this place at all since the blizzard stopped, he'll know I've been out there checking around. Of course I did it partly to see if I could get a sense of where he'd come from, or where he might be watching from. But I also did it to send the signal I was alert. To hold him off. But now I'm going to send a different signal. The new one is that I think we're safe now."

"So he'll feel safe making his approach?"

"Exactly. Like I said last night, I don't want to scare him off. Not now." His hands flexed a bit, as if he could feel them around Kevin's throat. "Tonight or tomorrow night, he's going to make his move. I'd bet money on it."

Kay drew an unsteady breath and looked down at her plate. She didn't think she could eat another mouthful. The moment she'd been both dreading and hoping for might only bc hours away.

Clint surprised her by reaching out to grasp her hand. "Trust me, Kay, he isn't as smart as he thinks he is. And he's not nearly as smart or capable as *you* think he is."

"Probably not."

"Trust me," he said again, and squeezed her hand. "If you can't eat that, I can get you something else."

She shook her head. "It's hard to swallow anything right now."

"Don't let fear overwhelm you. Use it, don't let it use you."

She wondered how many times he'd had to say that to someone and decided there were some things she didn't want to know. At lcast not tonight. "I'll try."

"Anger is a good substitute. If the fear gets to be too much, work up a good mad."

She smiled weakly. "That should be easy to do."

"Unless the fear takes charge."

She realized he was right about that. If ever she'd needed to be angry, now was it. But somehow fury kept slipping away before the force of memories. Memories of all the times Kevin had gotten to her despite her fleeing, despite locks, despite her going into hiding. And now he once again knew where she was.

So she looked at Clint, reminding herself of his strength, his confidence, his experience. He was a pillar, and she had to cling to that or slip away into the dark, icy waters of fear.

"You can do it, Kay," he said with the same calm confidence. "You figured out how to get away from him, and you ran with as much determination as I've ever seen. Despite a battered body, despite a concussion. You've got the right stuff."

That, she supposed, was a compliment. It *did* settle her a bit, and she was grateful. One thing she knew with absolute certainty. "He's not going to take me alive. Not again."

Clint's head jerked a little. "Have a little faith in me, woman."

"I do." In spite of herself, a small laugh escaped her. "I'm just saying."

"Well, that's okay, but it won't come to that."

Not as long as Clint was in one piece, maybe. But if Kevin came armed with a gun... A shudder shook her. "It's going to be bad," she whispered. "He *must* have a gun by now."

"Probably." It didn't seem to concern him at all. "And that's why you're going to be under the bed. If I get... momentarily disabled, you be sure to go for his ankles as soon as he gets close enough. Break them. He won't be expecting that."

This time it was *her* hands that clenched, feeling the weight of the tire iron that she would be holding. "I can do that," she said with conviction.

"Of course you can. And he's going to find me harder to put out of action than his worst nightmare."

His tone conveyed such certainty that she absolutely, completely believed him. He would know. He'd been there.

Something like calm passed through her and remained. With its arrival, fear seeped away. "Okay," she agreed, sounding firm for the first time. "But, Clint?"

"Yeah?"

"Don't let anything happen to yourself. We've got a few more rocket trips to take."

He laughed then, a genuine laugh. "Bet on it, lady. Bet on it."

Chapter 12

Night seeped into the house. Even with the lights on, Kay felt it. Night had always been a fearful time for her since Kevin, and she seemed as attuned to it as a mythical vampire. The thought almost amused her. If only she hadn't felt the fear seeping in with it.

At ten, after hours of pretending to read, she heard Clint stir.

"Time," he said. "I want you under the bed. Sorry the floor's so hard."

"I can take it."

And under the bed, perhaps she would feel safe in the darkness. She headed at once for the bedroom, carrying the tire iron with her. It hadn't been out of her reach all day.

Once there, she waited while Clint turned out lights one after another. Then he reached the bedroom and took her into his arms for one tight hug and a deep kiss. The kiss even managed to bypass her fear long enough to make her toes curl.

"Okay," he said huskily. "Get under the bed. Do you want a pillow or something?"

"It might get in the way." Still holding her weapon, she got down onto the floor and slipped beneath the bed. "Hey, Clint?"

"Yeah?"

"You're compulsive."

"Why do you say that?"

"Every self-respecting bed needs some dust bunnies. You don't have any."

The sound of his laugh cheered her. They were going to do this. Yes. Most definitely.

She had to believe that.

Then the bedroom light went out, too. She could tell he was still standing there for a moment; then he left the room on bare feet. Prowling. Much as she strained her ears, all she could hear was the crackle of the fire in the living room, and he'd even let that burn low.

She wiped her palms on the sweat suit and gripped the tire iron anew. Loosely, so her hands wouldn't cramp. Then quietly, slowly, she eased out from under the bed. She still lay on the floor beside it, so he couldn't see her as he walked by. But she knew one thing for certain—if Kevin got in here, Clint was not going to face him alone. She would never forgive herself.

Slowly her eyes adapted to the darkness. The little bit of orange glow that reached the room from the living room was enough. Just enough. If she had to go for Kevin's ankles, she would be able to see them. And she wouldn't miss.

She thought she heard Clint's voice murmuring quietly. Phone?

The floor was hard, especially where she was bruised, but she ignored it. Something filled her, something like a fierce pleasure. This time Kevin wouldn't catch her unawares. This time she was going to be ready. And if she had to use that tire iron, it was going to be a long time before he walked again.

And he deserved it. He was going to deserve everything he got when he came into this cabin. Because he had hurt her. Because he wanted to kill her. Because a man like that didn't deserve to walk around free.

Oh, yes, the anger was building. Slowly and surely, she was getting mad enough to seriously hurt someone.

She saw Clint's bare feet as he came into the room. "Clint?" she whispered.

"Yeah." He kept his voice low.

"Do you have your armor on?"

"Yes. Just put it on."

Something in his voice alerted her. "What happened?"

"I called Sarah."

"And?"

"The cops are close. Very close. They're tightening the noose right now."

"Oh, God…"

"Shh."

"Clint…"

"No more talking." His whisper was firm. "Not a sound, hear me?"

So she didn't make another sound. When she had to move, she did so as stealthily as she could, rising slowly to her feet, grasping the iron rod as she moved silently across the floor to stand just inside the bedroom door. If Kevin came this way, he was going to lose his face.

God, the waiting was endless. If the minutes crept by any slower, she would die of old age before dawn.

What was that?

She thought she'd heard a scratching from somewhere outside the room, but she was unable to tell any more than that. It could have come from anywhere. She held her breath and strained to hear, but the night was silent save for the distant crackling of the fire.

And then she thought she heard it again. Oh God. Her heart climbed into her throat. Dimly she saw Clint pad silently past the door, on his way toward his den—and the back door.

He'd heard something, too. Her heart nearly stopped. Once again she wiped her palms dry and gripped the tire iron. And once again she wished Clint had trusted her with a gun. What if he got hurt? What if she couldn't hit Kevin hard enough?

Clint's promises that nothing would stop him sounded weak now, even exaggerated.

But he would know, she reminded herself. He'd been wounded multiple times. If anyone could know what he was capable of, it was Clint.

She forced herself to quiet her breathing. To stand perfectly still. To wait, when waiting seemed impossible and every nerve in her felt stretched to the point of snapping.

Another sound, more like a snick. A lock? Her mind threw up images of Kevin slipping through the back door, invisible in the dark, bigger than Kevin had ever really been, some mythical, indestructible creature....

Stop! she screamed at herself silently and fought down the fear. *Don't let the fear use you. Use it.*

Good advice. The best advice. Adrenaline began to thrum through her, winding her tight. She could do this. She *would* do this. Because never, ever again was Kevin going to come after her.

"Over my dead body," she promised herself under her breath.

There it was, the faintest squeak of a hinge. The back door must be opening.

Why didn't Clint act? She squeezed her eyes shut for an instant, remembering the layout of the house. Of course, Clint wanted Kevin all the way inside, at least as far as the den door, where she suspected he was waiting.

Then he could take Kevin from the side.

It seemed like a brilliant plan. As long as Kevin didn't get off a shot. Because the idea that Clint might get hurt scared her more now than fear for herself.

The anger was strong in her now, making her ready, clearing her head until every sound, every sight, every thought, was as clear as if it were etched in glass.

Another squeak. The hinge? The sole of a shoe on the wood floor? She couldn't tell. All she knew was that the threat had entered the sanctuary of this house.

She bit her lip, barely daring to breathe.

Then it happened, so fast that her impressions were impossible to sort through. A thud. A grunt.

She stepped out into the hallway, weapon at the ready, and could make out two struggling figures, the bigger one undoubtedly Clint. She stepped closer, determined to hit Kevin with all her might the instant she could do it without hitting Clint. That man was going to pay.

Then the most fearsome sound of all—a gunshot.

She pressed closer, looking for an opportunity, but they were struggling together, both so close....

More grunts. Another shot.

God in heaven! She gripped the tire iron as tightly as she could, then watched in horror as the larger figure began to sink toward the floor.

He'd hurt Clint. The thought filled her with fury. Just a little closer, she thought. *A little closer, you bastard. A little closer.*

"There you are," said the all too familiar voice.

Panting hard now, she watched as he stepped over Clint. Oh God, Clint was dead.

Something in her snapped in that moment. She raced toward Kevin, screaming. Apparently her reaction startled him. He must have been expecting her to turn into the usual bundle of terrified passivity. But she didn't care anymore, didn't care about a damn thing except that was Kevin and he'd hurt Clint.

She swung the tire iron with all her might, wielding it with the power of all the terrified nights, all the anguish, all the pain, all the hatred she felt for him and what he had turned her into.

The iron bar connected with his forearm just as he was raising it, recovering enough to aim at her. She heard the satisfying crunch of bone, the yowl of pain, but, still maddened, she went after him again, this time catching him on his shoulder. She heard something heavy and metallic hit the floor, and then Kevin sagged, falling.

But just as she would have struck him again, Clint rose up behind Kevin and hurled himself at Kevin's back, knocking him over completely, driving the breath out of him.

Kevin shrieked as Clint rose up again, straddling him, lifting his head and banging in on the floor.

Clint and Kevin. Struggling on the floor.

"Light," Clint gasped. "Now!"

She ran a couple of steps down the hall and flipped the switch. And by the illumination of the overhead light, she could see that Clint was blood-soaked. His arm, the side of his face.

The fury that erupted in her went beyond anything she'd ever felt before. In an instant she became something more, or less, than human herself. She hardly felt the snarl that twisted her mouth. She had one aim and one aim only as she closed in on the men, waiting for her moment.

"Clint," she said in warning.

He pulled back just a bit, getting out of the way as the tire iron came down on Kevin's shoulder again. Hard. Kevin screamed. She raised the weapon again, ready to strike, but Clint's warning stopped her.

"No," he barked. "No. Stop."

She stood there, ready to kill, but Clint grabbed Kevin again, this time wrestling him onto his face. Kevin shrieked as if his shoulder were broken, but Clint ignored the sound. He shoved a hand into his pocket and pulled out a plastic tie. Ruthlessly he wrapped it around Kevin's wrists and locked it tight enough to evoke another howl.

Then, rearing back, he pulled out another tie and wrapped it around Kevin's ankles. Kevin howled again.

"Kay?" Clint's voice sounded a bit thin.

"What?"

"Call the cops now. The emergency number."

"But you're bleeding!" The true horror of that was beginning to penetrate, and rage began to give way to fear. A new kind of fear.

"Just call them!"

She dropped the tire iron and ran for the phone in the living room. 911 answered immediately, and she told them Clint was shot. A reassuring voice said, "They're on their way."

Message delivered, she went to unlock the front door. Then, numbly, she hurried back to the hallway. And Clint.

She didn't care about anything else right then.

He was sitting on the floor, leaning against the wall, knees up, staring at Kevin, who cried out every time he tried to struggle against his bonds.

Kevin saw Kay. "You bitch!" he spat. "You're going to pay for this!"

"Say that one more time," Clint growled, "and I will kill you with my bare hands right now."

The tone was so steely, so hard, that it left no room for doubt. Apparently even Kevin heard the death sentence there, and with an inarticulate sound of rage, he fell still.

Clint looked at Kay. "My belt. Now."

She knelt beside him swiftly, fought her way under the body armor and unbuckled his belt. Pulled it off.

"Wrap it around my arm above the wound and pull it as tight as you can. Now."

Her hands had begun to shake, making the task more difficult, but she managed it, even managed to ignore his groan when she yanked the belt tight and held it. "They're coming," she said breathlessly. "Clint, hang on. They're coming."

"My God!"

Kay turned and saw a woman with beautiful black hair, like a raven's wing, and wearing a deputy's uniform, standing in the bedroom doorway. Behind her was Micah, and beside him a man with a scarred face who looked as if he'd visited hell but had returned.

The woman immediately came over to Kay. "Are you all right?"

"Clint," Kay said. "Clint."

Then the man with the scarred face and Micah were pulling her to her feet and easing her away, then kneeling beside Clint. And Clint was looking pale, sweat beading his brow.

"Damn fool," Micah muttered as he yanked the belt even tighter.

"I'm okay," Clint said.

"Brachial artery," Micah said. "You could bleed out."

"I'll be fine, dammit!"

"Yeah, sure," said the man with the scarred face. "Just as soon as the bleeding stops and we get you a transfusion, then get the bullet out."

Kay sagged, and only the female deputy's grip saved her from collapse. "Clint," she said.

And somehow she managed to break loose and take two steps toward him. When she fell to the floor, she didn't care. She crawled the last few feet and pressed her head against his leg. "Clint."

A hand touched her hair. "I'll be fine, darlin'. I'll be fine."

"You better be, or I'll kill you."

Somebody laughed. She didn't know who, nor did she care. Because for some reason she seemed to be sinking into darkness.

She wasn't out for long. She woke to find EMTs checking her out. "I'm fine. The injuries are old. Clint?"

"He's being transported by air to the hospital," the man said. "He was still kicking and complaining when we took him out."

"Thank God." Her voice shook, and tears began to run down her face. "I need to get to him."

"I'll take you," the female deputy said. She squatted down beside Kay and smiled. "Hi, I'm Sarah Ironheart. You already met by brother-in-law, Micah."

"Yes. He's nice."

Sarah smiled. "I'll second that. And that scary guy over there?"

Kay turned her head and saw the man with the scarred face standing over the bed where EMTs were checking out Kevin.

"That's our sheriff, Gage Dalton. He takes it personally when someone like Kevin hurts someone in this county. I think he's already called the Feds in, too."

"I wanted to kill him," Kay admitted, looking at Kevin and realizing he no longer seemed mythically powerful. In fact, he looked downright puny.

"I'm not surprised," Sarah said. "There are a few of us who would gladly have done it for you after we heard what he'd done."

"Clint wouldn't let me."

Micah turned and looked at her with ebony eyes. "Clint's a wise man. You don't want to live with that."

He would know. She remembered him saying he'd killed his wife's ex-husband to protect her.

Assured that Kevin was well-guarded now, Kay let her eyes close, let go of one terrible tension and gave in to a new one. "Clint," she said again.

"Come on," Sarah said. "Let's see if you can stand. Then we'll follow them to the hospital."

The drive to the hospital seemed endless, though of course it wasn't. Sarah understood her need for quiet, though, and didn't try to converse.

Kay herself was wrapped in the memory of those nightmare minutes from when Kevin had entered the house to when she had crawled to Clint's side. He had to be all right. He *had* to. Her fists clenched on her lap, and she willed the car to fly.

But even at the hospital, she couldn't see him. He'd already been taken to surgery. Sarah waited with her, bringing her coffee.

"Clint's tough," the other woman said at one point. "He'll make it, Kay."

"He's human," she answered. Her eyes felt swollen with unshed tears, hot and burning. "He's only human."

Sarah squeezed her shoulder and let it lie. "We'll need to talk to you in depth. Later. When you're ready."

Kay managed a jerky nod. At the moment she doubted she could manage a simple coherent sentence. All she wanted to know was that Clint was all right.

Dawn was just breaking through the windows in the waiting room when a young doctor finally approached. He looked tired, but not upset, and Kay felt the first ray of hope in hours.

"Clint's fine," he said before she could ask. Then he sat beside her and looked at her. "I'm going to treat you as next of kin, because that's what he was demanding when they brought him in. He's in recovery. The bullet nicked the brachial artery in his arm. The blood loss was bad enough, but probably not as bad as it looked, okay?"

She nodded, unable to speak.

"He's going to be a hundred percent fine in no time. In fact, we should be able to release him tomorrow, if we know he has care at home."

"I'll take care of him."

The doctor nodded. "He needs some time to wake up, then I'll have someone come get you and take you to him."

"Thank you." Relief washed over her so strongly that she had to lean forward and put her head between her knees. God, what was wrong with her?

The doctor touched her shoulder. "You've been beaten, haven't you?"

"A few days ago."

"Then I want someone to take a look at you. I don't like that bruise on your head."

"I'm fine!"

"You sound just like Clint."

"I can't afford it, anyway. I don't have insurance."

"That doesn't matter here. Let someone take a look at you. It'll help pass the time until you can see Clint."

So she let Sarah lead her away to an examining room, where another young doctor, who introduced himself as David Marcus, checked her from head to toe. And Sara took photos.

She didn't care anymore how many photos were taken of her purpling, green and black bruises.

All she wanted was Clint.

"Well," said Dr. Marcus finally, "I wouldn't have believed it, but you seem to be fine."

"That's what I said."

He gave her a smile that penetrated the blanket of fog that seemed to layer her mind, a fog that allowed only concern for Clint to penetrate. "I doubt you were as fine a couple of days ago. But it's good to know we don't seem to have anything to worry about."

She let that little bit of offered warmth wrap around her heart.

At long last they took her to Clint. He was lying on a bed, his arm bandaged from shoulder to elbow, and held to his side by gauze wrapping. He had more color now, she noted, as she sank into the chair beside the bed.

Then, carefully, she reached out and took his hand. His eyes fluttered open. "Kay?"

"I'm fine," she said. "Sleep."

His eyes closed again, and she laid her head on the pillow beside his, still clinging to his hand. She let fatigue claim her then. Her guardian angel was safe, and nothing else mattered.

Sometime during the afternoon, she woke. Lifting her head slowly, blinking, she found herself looking into Clint's gray eyes.

"How are you?" he asked.

"I'm fine. You were the one who got shot."

"It's nothing. I'm ready to get out of here."

"Not until tomorrow," she said firmly. "At the earliest."

One corner of his mouth lifted. "Afraid you can't handle me?"

Her jaw dropped a little, and then she started to smile. "I think I can handle you. But I want what's best for you."

"And that means getting out of here. I'm all stitched up. I want..." He hesitated. "Well, maybe I want too much."

What could he possibly mean? She drew her brows together. "What?"

"I want," he said, his voice low, "to be somewhere we can talk."

"Oh." Probably because telling her she would have to move on soon wouldn't be easy to do when a nurse could come walking in at any moment. Well, she thought, as her heart squeezed with pain, did she want to delay that another twenty-four hours, or did she want to face it now?

Either way, it was going to practically kill her.

"They won't let you go," she said finally.

"Actually, they can't stop me."

"Umm...there's this whole transportation thing, Clint. No car."

"Hell." He sighed.

At that moment the sheriff—Gage Dalton, she seemed to remember—limped in. He was smiling crookedly, one side of his face seeming to have lost some mobility to the burn scar that marred it. "Well, well, the hero's awake."

"I'm no hero," Clint grumped. "Cut that out."

"I thought it was a damn good operation," Gage remarked. "We were only a couple of minutes away at the critical point. And we got the guy."

"I hope he's hurting."

Gage's smile widened as he limped to the other chair and dragged it closer. "He's definitely hurting. We've got him cuffed to a bed down the hall. Broken shoulder, broken collarbone, broken ankle. Plenty of bruises and cuts. Somebody did a number on him."

"Thank the Valkyrie here," Clint said, nodding toward Kay. "I think she'd had enough."

"Evidently so." Gage's gaze turned to Kay. "We've been working while you were hiding. Do you want to know?"

"Please."

"Well, we got his priors. We got the other complaints you filed against him. I still don't understand why he kept getting away with it."

"Some cops," Clint remarked, "have too much on their plates to worry about one little lady."

"Evidently so. Lack of evidence." Gage snorted. "They could have had it with some effort. We got it." He looked at Kay. "You can't exactly travel cross country and leave no trail at all. Anyway, I thought you'd like to know he's being charged with stalking, multiple batteries, attempted murder, kidnapping—which will probably be handled by the Feds, since he took you across state lines—and I don't think he's going to breathe free air for the rest of his days."

Relief caused her to sag as every bone in her body seemed to turn to rubber. "Thank God," she whispered. "Thank God."

"Then, of course, there's the attempted murder of Clint, a second attempted murder charge for you, breaking and entering of a domicile… The prosecutor is having a field day with this one. If it's in the books, he's going to get charged with it."

"Good!"

Gage smiled, clearly satisfied. "Clint? Still sure you don't want to be deputized?"

"No thanks, I like my life."

In that, Kay heard the death knell of her hopes. Feeling crushed, she hoped only she didn't show it.

"Well, I've got some more good news," Gage continued. "The doc says you can go home now, if you promise to be good—and if you have a nurse." He arched a brow at Kay. "Will you mind being a nurse?"

She started to smile. "It's the least I can do."

"That's settled, then. We can take your statements in a couple of days." Gage pushed himself out of the chair, a faint grimace of pain crossing his face. "I'll get someone in here to help you get dressed, Clint. Then I'll take you both home."

Chapter 13

Home. Gage had used the word so easily the day when he had taken them to Clint's place from the hospital. But it would never be her home, Kay thought sadly. Even as she took joy in every little thing Clint let her do for him as his arm healed, she knew this would be the last time she could do anything for him.

He liked his life the way it was. He'd said so.

Since he couldn't yet move easily enough to get in and out of bed, he'd settled grumbling into life on the couch. Clearly a man who didn't like being unable to do exactly what he wanted when he wanted, he put up with being an invalid as if it were the worst thing in the world.

Finally she snapped at him, "It *could* be worse, you know. You might be dead."

At that he laughed, surprising her, and tried to give in with good grace when he needed help, much as it went against his nature.

But the third afternoon, when he seemed to have recovered from his surgery and the loss of blood, when he started to look bright-eyed again, he asked her to come sit beside him on the couch.

This was it, she thought. He was going to tell her he could manage without her. And he probably could, even if being temporarily short an arm hindered him.

So she sat beside him, on his uninjured side, and waited for him to lower the boom. Her chest ached with the awareness that grief was approaching.

"I'm awful," he said.

Startled, she looked at him. "What in the world are you talking about?"

"I'm awful."

She frowned at him. "Would you like to clarify that?"

"I'm talking about the kind of person I am."

"Well, I beg to differ."

"You've only seen part of me."

"I've seen more than you think. Do you honestly think I don't see the ghosts in your eyes? The predator you can become?"

It was his turn to look shocked. Then he said, "I've seen and done some pretty horrible things. Things I couldn't tell you in a million years."

"We're entitled to some secrets." One corner of her mouth quivered. Rejection came in all forms, and apparently Clint was trying a different version. She just hoped she had a chance of fighting it.

"Some secrets are corrosive. They eat at the soul."

She didn't try to argue. Her throat was so tight it hurt, and she didn't know how to argue with this, anyway. So she waited, fingers twined together so tightly they ached.

He sighed and closed his eyes momentarily. "Okay," he said. "I've been a bad guy more often than not."

"In your own estimation."

"That's the only one that matters."

Again she couldn't argue, nor could she tell him how much it hurt to hear him talk about himself this way.

"I came to hide in this place so I could try to work things through. So I could avoid being a bad guy again."

When he didn't continue, she said softly, "Tell me."

He paused, as if trying to find a way to make sure she understood. "When you've been a trained killer, when you've been at war too much and too often, things inside you get a little broken. I don't trust myself."

"Why?"

"Because I've seen some of the best men I know find it impossible to come back to civilian life. Because when it hits them, they take their pain, their rage, out on their families. We're not fit for the regular world anymore."

"You *believe* that, but—"

"I've seen it. Believing has nothing to do with it."

She nodded, beginning to truly grasp his problem. "But, Clint, have you ever gone off like that on a friend? Or a lover?"

He jaw tightened. "Not yet. But it helps that I stay solitary."

"Maybe."

"There's no maybe about it. I don't put myself in situations where the beast could get loose."

"Except to protect a woman who landed on your doorstep."

He passed his hand over his face. "You saw what I became."

"I saw what *I* became. You're the only thing that kept me from killing Kevin."

"I didn't want you to have that on your conscience."

"And you didn't kill him, either."

"I wanted to," he murmured. "Oh, God, how I wanted to."

"But you didn't. And I wanted to, but you stopped me. That ought to tell you something."

"Kay, don't you understand? I'm trying to tell you that you can't trust me!"

"And I'm trying to tell you that I already do! Completely. Implicitly. Like it or not, Clint Ardmore, I trust you. And I have every confidence in your self-control."

He looked at her again, doubtfully, then almost fearfully. "I'm afraid of taking advantage of you."

"In what way?"

"You're free of Kevin now. You could go out there and have a whole glorious life. Instead you're sitting here beside me, a crusty old hermit. You should go and try your new wings. And not let me take advantage of you."

She twisted a little so she was looking directly at him. "How are you taking advantage of me?"

"You were dependent on me for a while. It creates feelings in you that might not be real."

Her heart sped up. She didn't know whether she was angry or feeling the first stirrings of hope. All she knew was that this was one fight she intended to win. "Do you really think I'm that stupid?"

"You're not stupid at all!"

"So you keep saying. I'm also not a princess who's spent her life in a tower. I've had enough experience to know a few things. And one of the things I know is that you're a good, a *very* good man."

"No."

"Yes." She rose up on her knees and put her face close to his. "I know I've been looking for you, just you, my entire life."

"You can't know that."

"I already do. You have absolutely no idea what you've done for me, and I'm not talking about Kevin. You've made me feel worthwhile again. You've made me feel smart, not dumb. You've given me back a kind of confidence I haven't had since I was a kid, and all because *you* thought I mattered enough to shake up your routine and take a huge risk with your own life. To talk to me like an intelligent adult. To care for me when I was almost helpless." She grabbed his shirtfront, taking care not to jar his wounded arm. "Don't you see? Not since I was a kid has anyone cared that way for me. Not since I was a kid has anyone thought I was worth even a smidgeon of that kind of effort."

"But..."

She shook her head, silencing him. "Throw me out and go back to your solitude if you want. But no matter what you do, you can't prevent me from being in love with you."

"In love?" he repeated in an almost-whisper, and closed his eyes. "How can you know that? How can you be sure?"

"Try this," she said fiercely. "I ran more than once. I could have run from you the instant the blizzard was over. I could have called the cops and told them to come get me. I was *never* as helpless as you seem to think."

"You couldn't run. No money. No place to go."

"Dammit, I've always found a way to run. I've spent my whole life running. I would have figured something out within a day if I had wanted to. I wasn't your prisoner!"

He opened his eyes, his gaze boring into hers. Finally a long, unsteady sigh escaped him. "You mean that?"

"Of course I mean it. I ran from a killer. Do you think I couldn't have run from you? Listen, Clint, please. I mean it. I love you. I trust you. If you don't trust me, that's fine. If you want to give this a trial run for six months, a year, ten years, fine. Whatever it takes to make you comfortable. Because the one thing on this earth that I absolutely do not want to do is walk out your door for good."

A few seconds passed in silence, and then she saw something new blazing in his eyes. Something bright and beautiful.

"Ghosts are hard to live with," he said.

"I'll live with them. You may have noticed, I have some of my own."

"And you'll leave if ever you want to?"

"I always have."

He started to smile, the stony facade giving way piece by piece. "I love you," he said. "I love you, Kay Young."

"I love *you*, Clint Ardmore. Now, are you done trying to get rid of me?"

His smile broadened. "I give up."

"Good." She settled back on the couch and leaned against his shoulder. Her heart began to do a happy tap-dance of joy. He wasn't going to get rid of her.

"In fact," he said slowly, "I want to marry you."

She caught her breath as joy surged in her. "When?"

"I don't want to rush you." But his voice held a tentative note of happiness.

"Next week would be fine," she said.

Suddenly it was as if he'd never been wounded at all. With one arm he lifted her onto his lap and kissed her hungrily, deeply.

A forever kind of kiss. Because they'd both found their forever kind of home.

* * * * *

COMING NEXT MONTH

Available June 29, 2010

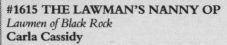

ROMANTIC SUSPENSE

HARLEQUIN®

A Romance

FOR EVERY MOOD™

Spotlight on

Heart & Home

Heartwarming romances
where love can happen
right when you least expect it.

See the next page to enjoy a sneak peek
from Silhouette Special Edition®,
a Heart and Home series.

Introducing McFARLANE'S PERFECT BRIDE
by USA TODAY *bestselling author Christine Rimmer,*
from Silhouette Special Edition®.

Entranced. Captivated. Enchanted.

Connor sat across the table from Tori Jones and couldn't help thinking that those words exactly described what effect the small-town schoolteacher had on him. He might as well stop trying to tell himself he wasn't interested. He was powerfully drawn to her.

Clearly, he should have dated more when he was younger.

There had been a couple of other women since Jennifer had walked out on him. But he had never been entranced. Or captivated. Or enchanted.

Until now.

He wanted her—*her*, Tori Jones, in particular. Not just someone suitably attractive and well-bred, as Jennifer had been. Not just someone sophisticated, sexually exciting and discreet, which pretty much described the two women he'd dated after his marriage crashed and burned.

It came to him that he...he *liked* this woman. And that was new to him. He liked her quick wit, her wisdom and her big heart. He liked the passion in her voice when she talked about things she believed in.

He liked *her.* And suddenly it mattered all out of proportion that she might like him, too.

Was he losing it? He couldn't help but wonder. Was he cracking under the strain—of the soured economy, the McFarlane House setbacks, his divorce, the scary changes in his son? Of the changes he'd decided he needed to make in his life and himself?

Strangely, right then, on his first date with Tori Jones, he didn't care if he just might be going over the edge. He was having a great time—having *fun,* of all things—and he didn't want it to end.

Is Connor finally able to admit his feelings to Tori, and are they reciprocated?
Find out in McFARLANE'S PERFECT BRIDE
by USA TODAY bestselling author Christine Rimmer.
Available July 2010,
only from Silhouette Special Edition®.